The Clutches of
Mimi Bouchard

The Clutches of Mimi Bouchard

John Travis

Book cover artwork by SHU YAMAMOTO
Licensed by MEW MEOW PRODUCTION

ISBN number: 978-1-7398195-8-3

Printed and Bound by 4Edge

Published by:

Head Shot
85 Gertrude Road
Norwich
UK

editorheadshot@gmail.com
www.headshotpress.com

For Ian Alexander Martin, who took a chance on me when no-one else would, and in memory of Cassie (?1996-2013), a crazy pooch with killer eyebrows whose fussy eating habits provided me with one of the first Benji Spriteman ideas.

'Like I give a Rat's ass,' said the Chihuahua in the gaudy checked jacket. 'See ya later, Spriteman.'

Later.

For the longest time I wanted it to be later, a later where I was alive, a later where I wouldn't have time to think because life would be one long rollercoaster ride, a headlong rush into the wind that threatened to rip the fur from my body, a later where I'd be hanging on by the skin of my teeth and loving every second of it.

Later.

And then out of the blue, that later came along.

Be careful what you wish for.

Yeah, it's funny how things work out sometimes. Still, I'll be okay.

But I'm getting ahead of myself. I need to tell you how all this got started, on a quiet, rainy day a few weeks ago. They were all quiet days then; had been for months. I spent most of my time asleep, occasionally nudged into life by the ringing of the phone or the sound of the rain beating against my window or Taki coming in, usually with a cup of coffee for me to fall asleep next to. But that day two of these things happened one right after the other; the rain on the window followed by an appearance by Taki. Only this time instead of coffee my secretary burst in with a phrase, the like of which I'd rarely heard before…

One: Past – Imperfect

1.

'Goddamn fishwife!' she yelled, slamming my door shut behind her.

Barely awake, I was trying to convince myself that the noise at my back was the sound of raindrops hitting the window and not ball bearings colliding with a tin roof. Dropping the idea, I lifted my head from my desk and was just about to ask her what the matter was when I saw for myself. Jerking back in shock, my outstretched arm caught the edge of my half-full coffee cup and sent it scudding across the desk onto the floor, leaving a great black pool on my largely empty desk in its wake. A split second later a gust of wind smashed the window inwards so hard that the glass almost broke when the frame hit the wall. Locking the window, I could hear the cup spinning on the floor and my secretary breathing heavily through her nostrils. I looked at her again. Or rather someone who once resembled her.

Thinking that I'd woken up in a nightmare, I said the only thing I could in such circumstances.

'Huh?'

'Is that all you've got to say?' she screeched, pointing at herself so violently I thought she was going to stab herself in the head with one of her claws. 'Look at me! *Look what they did to my fur!'*

It was at that moment I noticed the wetness in the leg of my pants. My desk, never level at the best of times, was fine when it was covered in paper; but apparently when it was covered in coffee the coffee ran down a slight slope towards the animal sitting, or, in this case, standing behind it. Taking a handkerchief from my pocket, I patted myself down.

'Um, you've been to the Salon,' I said, wringing out the handkerchief into the waste basket. 'But you don't appear to be very happy about it.'

'Yes, I *have* been to the salon,' Taki informed me after getting a towel from her office and mopping my desk with it. 'And how would you feel, Benji, if you'd just spent a half weeks' wages there and ended up looking like this – would *you* be happy?'

The desk now dry, I gave her the once-over.

One of the first things I'd noticed about Taki the day she walked into my office a few years earlier, initially as a client before becoming my secretary, were her eyes – a brilliant icy blue, made even icier by the abundance of white fur surrounding them. But now those eyes weren't so icy any more, and that was because of the change in her fur; instead of the usual pure white, it was now a shocking bright red. I liked the bright red too, and I didn't really mind whether it was piled up high or combed down flat, but I think it's nice to have consistency in such matters. Unfortunately for Taki, it looked like her stylist didn't agree.

'It looks like you've been battered with a rolling pin,' I said, pointing to the flat side.

'Had the cheek to tell me it would spring up in a day or two,' she muttered, pacing up and down.

'But why –'

'*Why?* That's what I wanted to know!' she snapped, paws planted on her hips as she faced me. 'But I couldn't get an answer. And that's when *she* came out, all sweetness and light.'

'The big boss lady?'

'Jumped-up madam. '"*Oh my dear paws, what's all this noise out here?*"' Taki said in an exaggerated drawl. '"*Is someone not satisfied? My dear, the rain will work its magic on that in no time.*" And before I knew what was happening I was being ushered out of the place and the door was slammed behind me. And when I turned back it had a "Closed" sign on it.'

'So you paid in advance,' I said.

'*What?*'

'If she escorted you from the premises straight after it happened you must have paid in advance. You said it cost you half a weeks' wages.'

On the edge of my desk I keep a telephone directory. Putting one of her paws on top of it, I thought for a split second she was going to pick it up and hurl it at me.

'As I was saying,' she continued, the ice in her eyes turning to fire, 'there was suddenly a "Closed" sign in the window. But according to their opening times they weren't due to close for hours. And that's when the screaming started.'

'Which you've decided to carry on with here.'

'*Not me, her!* She sounded half crazy – things were getting thrown around, some of the stylists were crying – she went from nice as pie to a screeching banshee inside a few seconds. Well I tell you, I won't be going *there* again!'

As it was my day for saying stupid things I decided to keep at it. 'So why go at all?' I asked.

'Oh, because I'd heard good things about it,' she said, her anger losing its edge. 'The area around it's a dump but the place itself is nice enough. It's just some of the staff leave something to be desired, that's all.' Taking her paw off the directory, she grabbed the coffee cup off the floor and took it through to the sink in reception, her lopsided fur swaying as she went.

When she came back in a few minutes later with more coffee, she'd somehow managed to plaster the sprung-up side of her fur down so it was roughly level with the flat side. It didn't look too bad, but I knew better than to say so.

'I see you've had another busy day of it,' she said, bumping the cup down on my desk.

'It'll pick up,' I told her, yawning.

Waiting until the door was closed and I could hear the sounds of cups being washed in the sink, I put my head back on my arms and closed my eyes once more.

'Fishwife,' I muttered to myself before dozing off.

I couldn't see it at the time, but I was stagnating, getting flabby; and The Terror – that fateful night when the world changed forever – now seemed decades ago instead of a little over forty months. After it happened it seemed like anything was possible; one day we were crawling along the ground on all fours, the next standing tall, masters of all we surveyed, savouring the freedoms that the soon-to-be extinct Human Race had taken for granted. And later when things calmed down, we took over their homes and jobs as well; in my case, the Spriteman Detective Agency, sorting out the various problems of the animals that came to my office, a steady trickle of surveillance jobs, unfaithful spouses and assorted missing creatures, occasionally punctuated by something a bit juicier. But after my last big case about a year ago the trickle became a dribble and then just the odd drop, which meant a lot of sitting around doing nothing. And it wasn't just my gut that was in need of some fine-tuning – the stuff between my ears was turning into jelly too, and the only thing I did that provided any stimulation – if you could call it that – was driving around the city at night.

Sooner or later, something had to give.

The process started a few days later, during a game of cards.

'There you go,' Taki said, marching into my office and slapping a sheaf of papers down in front of me, sending the cards flying. 'From Linus. Hot off the press.'

I scowled up at her; for once I'd been winning. Unperturbed, she scowled back. 'I think you should read it,' she said. 'Now.'

As far as I knew nothing important was due, just a report on the tailing job the Mouse had been carrying out, the kind of case I detested. But her scowl said she wasn't going to leave until I'd read it. With a shrug, I picked up the report and began to read:

SURVEILLANCE REPORT FOR BENJAMIN
SPRITEMAN, HEAD OF THE SPRITEMAN
DETECTIVE AGENCY, INTO THE ACTIVITIES OF
ERROL MORRIS, AS INSTIGATED BY GLENYS
RATMAN ('SPOUSE'), AND ACTED UPON BY LINUS
SPAYLEY (OPERATIVE)

CLIENT NAME: RATMAN, GLENYS
CASE NO: GR1-215-SDA/LS-103
DATE: 21/10 (Year 4)
TIME OF CALL: 2.42 PM

On the date and time mentioned above, a phone call was received by the Agency from Ms Ratman expressing concern regarding her common-law partner, Mr Morris. Ms Ratman, becoming increasingly suspicious of Mr Morris's reasons/excuses for coming home late on certain nights of the week (namely Mondays, Wednesdays and Thursdays), was of the opinion that Mr Morris was conducting an affair, or series of affairs, on said evenings with female of females unknown in his office at the Zabriskie Wireless Company. Following a face-to-face meeting with the client later that afternoon, and, after the usual terms and conditions etc. were discussed, it was agreed that I would conduct an investigation into Mr Morris's activities.

Learning that Mr Morris usually left home for work each day around 8.30am, I began my surveillance outside the Morris/Ratman residence at 8.00am the following morning. At 8.28am Mr Morris emerged from his home, so I followed on foot at a discreet distance as he took the 24-minute walk to his office on 37th street. It is my firm belief that the object of this surveillance was unaware he was being followed.

Arriving at his place of work at 8.52am, he stopped for several minutes to talk to the Dog on the door before entering, during which time I took the first of several pictures of Mr Morris (see overleaf). At 8.57am Mr Morris went inside, and I decamped to the café opposite the Wireless Company, which afforded me a clear view of the office's comings and goings.

When the subject appeared again at 12.57pm among several other animals presumably on their lunch break, I had the perfect opportunity to follow him without being spotted. Leaving the café, I-

Turning the page, I found myself looking at a snapshot of a very plain-looking carrot-cruncher standing before a set of glass doors, talking to a German Shepherd in a peaked cap.

Casting a quick look at Taki, I decided against saying what was on my mind and instead thumbed through the rest of the document, all fourteen pages of it, not including photographs, until I could contain myself no longer.

'So the Rabbit was playing away from home,' I said. 'I daresay Ms Ratman's not too happy about that, but she got the service she asked for and paid up. End of story.'

But Taki wasn't about to let it go. 'But what about the *report*?' she asked.

I thought about it. 'Well, it seems fairly typical. It's way too long, but that's just how the Mouse does things. He likes to put the effort in.'

'*Yes!*' Taki said, banging on the desk. 'Exactly: *He likes to put the effort in.* Whereas you –' stopping herself, she looked away.

'Oh, I don't, is that it? Forgive me, but you seem to have forgotten who's in charge around here.'

'"In charge"? That's a joke! Me and the Mouse run around doing all the work while you sit in here on your fat ass playing solitaire!'

A long angry pause followed on both sides. That stung, and she knew it.

It was maybe just as well that the phone rang when it did. Storming back to her part of the office, Taki went to answer it.

Whoever it was, I never found out. The call never came through to me.

I stayed angry at her for the rest of the day. Not that she knew that; as far as I know, she never came into my office again. Then again, I did spend most of the afternoon asleep, in preparation for my nightly drive.

And that's when the dam *really* broke.

*

Of all the freedoms which the animal population has enjoyed since The Terror struck, one of the most popular – at least to those of us without feathers, and let's face it, most of *them* have an even better way to travel – is driving. Me, I started late – for various reasons I didn't much fancy it, but about a year ago I finally bit the bullet and learned, hoping that the ability to get from A to B and back again quicker than before would help me finish cases faster and perhaps give me time to take on new ones; unfortunately, this was around the same time my workload started to drop off.

They're long days when you're sitting at your desk waiting for the phone to ring; and like most Cats given the chance there's a real possibility that said wait is at some point going to turn into a nap; in some respects at least we haven't changed *that* much. Consequently, after a day spent dozing I'd leave the office wide awake, craving something, *anything* that wasn't sitting around waiting for a phone to ring.

So I drove, prowling the night-time streets like some Old Tom Cat from Pre-Terror days but now in a car, down the main streets, along dark, dank alleys, through long-deserted districts full of nothing but dust and ghosts.

You see a lot of strange things when you drive around a city at night. But mostly you see lights: lights from apartment blocks and offices, red, pink, and blue neon lights hanging above seedy nightclubs, lights from advertising hoardings; I liked to see these lights. And when I saw places that didn't have any lights, I used to shine mine on them, so bored had I become. And because of this silly little ritual I came across something that was to trouble me for weeks to come.

On my way back home one night after several hours' cruising the streets, I found myself approaching the rear entrance to an old apartment block I'd driven past many times before. It was several storeys high, and dotted with windows. Below each window was a section of the great hulking metal staircase that was bolted to the length and breadth of the wall.

For the first time that I could remember, not a single light was on in any of those back windows.

Deciding I'd remedy this, I drove into the entrance of the parking lot, where, with the exception of a few cars in front of me, I had an almost perfect view of the back wall. Turning off my engine and putting my lights on full beam, the whole back side of the building was suddenly awash in crisp, bright light, bringing the staircase into sharp relief; and smack bang in the centre of it was the huge, imposing shadow of a Toucan, stretching up towards the roof. I knew it was a Tuke because the beak was so big, its bulk extending across most of the back wall, the tip over to the left.

For the blink of an eye it was still. Then it happened, the thing which cut its way through the lethargy I'd been experiencing for so long: a sudden, sharp movement of the head towards the ground, with the beak lunging forwards like a huge misshapen knife. Because of the other cars in the lot I wasn't able to see what it had lunged at; then the head appeared again and momentarily the shadow got bigger, presumably as the Tuke headed towards the entrance; then finally it shrank as it was sucked in through the door, then it was gone.

My heart jackhammering, I tried to take in what I'd just seen when a voice from the building suddenly called out:

'Hey, turn that light out, can't you!'

That voice was the final straw. In panic I killed the lights, backed the car out of the lot and roared off, not remembering to turn my lights on again until I was halfway home.

It was when I was lying in bed later that I finally realised how far I'd fallen. What had I witnessed? What had the Tuke lunged at? Had a crime been committed? Maybe, maybe not. But *whatever* I'd seen it had spooked me. And worse still, I knew that had the same thing happened even a few months earlier I'd have gone into that apartment block, no matter how spooked I was, just to find out what the hell it was that'd happened, because I was nosey like that. Instead, I ran away from it.

And sometimes you have to face your fears head on.

For the next week or so my mind kept going back to that night, that image of the lunging beak. What had I seen? And equally perplexing, what did it *remind* me of? It felt strangely like a warning, but about what I had no idea. And while I was thinking about all this I waited, waited for a case – any case – promising myself that I'd see it through to the bitter end, no matter how boring it was, so I could prove to myself that I still had it.

So one evening when a rather odd couple came to my office with a case that promised little, it seemed ideal. And I took it on.

But I'll be okay.

Two: Present – Tense

2.

I was shaken from my daydreaming by a knock at the door, which I could just about hear over the sound of squabbling.

'Come in.'

'Someone here to speak to you,' Taki said, standing on the threshold to my office, eyeing me disdainfully. 'Two of them actually. As you can no doubt tell.'

'Yes,' I said, just about managing to meet her gaze after a week of trying to get back in her good books, 'well, send them in.'

'With pleasure,' she said, the row behind her getting louder. As she moved aside, two midgets bustled into my office, and Taki slammed my door shut after them. Not that the mutt and the moggy in front of me noticed; they were still too busy arguing.

They weren't midgets really – the canine was about five-two and the feline a few inches shorter than that. She'd probably have been about the same size he was if her ears hadn't been squashed flat.

'Um, take a seat,' I said during a lull in their noise. Looking at his companion, the Dog gestured towards a chair with his paw. Once she was seated, he flopped down in the seat next to her.

They were certainly a strange pair – the Dog a white Chihuahua/Jack Russell crossbreed with patches of thick reddish fur, very large ears, a delicate-looking skull and a weeping left eye (a common trait with Chihuahuas), the Cat a Shorthaired ginger Tabby with the aforementioned ears who looked like she wanted nothing more than to vanish in a puff of smoke. Sensing that the former did most of the talking, I addressed him.

'So what can I do for you, Mr –'

'Chomsky,' he informed me. 'Willie Chomsky. This is Sascha, my sister –' he jerked a claw roughly in her direction, '– and what you can do for us is get the goddamned Queen of Sheba off our backs.'

I couldn't think of anything to say. Luckily, I didn't have to.

'We run the Pawnbroker's on Montcrieff Terrace – Chomsky's Pawnbrokers,' Sascha explained.

'Yeah, and we don't sell crap either, despite what she says,' the Chihuahua put in angrily. 'Anyway, the reason we're here is because –'

'She killed him,' Sascha said in a small voice. 'She killed our brother.'

I looked at each of them in turn. 'Perhaps you'd better start from the beginning,' I suggested.

'Oh, I intend to,' Chomsky told me, folding his arms across his chest.

'We'll have to make it quick, Willard,' Sascha put in, tapping her wristwatch with a claw. 'Because we still have to… you know…'

'Have to what?' "Willard" snapped.

'We still have to… *pick up something*,' she said testily. 'Remember?'

'Oh! Yeah,' he said a couple of seconds later. 'Okay, Spriteman – the quick version. What happened was this–'

I was glad all I got was the quick version, because it meant that the next time I saw them I could get the full story and hopefully take it in without getting too distracted by the way the pair of them looked. I caught little bits – something about a Salon and a sign and somebody called Krukowski and someone else called Butler and the 'goddamned mansion' the Queen of Sheba owned out of town – enough anyway to make me suspect that the whole thing was little more than a petty neighbourhood dispute. And because of this I found myself more interested in the appearances of the creatures sitting opposite me than the tale they were telling.

First of all it was Chomsky's jacket, a hideous patchwork quilt of yellow and dark brown checks, which despite its apparent age and faded appearance was still incredibly loud. Luckily for him, his voice was even louder – a grating, urgent weasily whine; the kind of voice I imagined would stay in my head for hours after I'd heard it. Which is what happened.

After that it was the cigarette, although if it hadn't been for the smell of tobacco and the constant stream of smoke drifting up towards his face, I'd have sworn the spindly object hanging from the side of his mouth was a twig. Presumably he rolled them himself, and judging by the colour of his paws – and to a lesser extent the fur on his face, both a stained, sick-room yellow – he got through a lot of them. I'd heard stories about animals whose fur had turned yellow because they smoked too much, but this was the first time I'd actually seen it for myself. I wondered if all the smoking was the real reason his eye kept weeping, a thin dribble of brown-black goo oozing towards the yellow fur below. After a while the goo began to irritate me, so I rubbed at my right eye, hoping the gesture would prompt him do the same; when he didn't I had to look away, and turned my attention instead to his sister – the familial connection being a hangover from days of ownership, and not blood related.

Sascha Chomsky was almost his polar opposite; polite, perfectly still, and on the few occasions she did voice an opinion she did it quietly, all the while sitting with her paws folded one on top of the other in her lap. The word 'timid' could have been invented for her. The flat ears didn't help; it looked like someone had gotten hold of them and scrunched them into her ear canals. And although it didn't seem to affect her hearing, it helped give the impression that Sascha wouldn't say boo to a Goose even if the Goose had given its express permission. But despite or perhaps because of this, there was something about her I found oddly unnerving.

A couple of minutes into Chomsky's speech she looked at her watch and tugged her brother's arm. 'Willard, we have to go,' she said.

'Look, come over to the shop tomorrow morning,' Chomsky said as they rose from their chairs. 'We can explain it properly then.'

'I can't believe you *forgot!*' Sascha hissed at him as they headed for the door. By the time they'd reached reception, they'd started bickering again. Hearing noise in the street below a minute or so later, I looked out of the window and saw them standing before a car, still arguing.

A glance at the clock on the wall said it was 6.15: time to go. All of a sudden I felt glad to be leaving. Turning out my light, I walked into reception.

It was a surprise to find Taki still there. 'They quarrel worse than us,' I said.

'Are you going to take it?' she asked.

'I'm going to take it.'

She shrugged, half smiled. 'That's good. And thank you.'

'For what?' I said, returning the half smile.

'The lift to the bus depot you're about to give me. Much appreciated.'

'Bus depot it is,' I said, gesturing for her to lead the way.

In the car neither of us said much, although I sensed for one of us it was just a matter of waiting for the right moment. Apparently that was as I pulled up at the bus depot. 'Did I hear the name "Bouchard" mentioned in the office earlier?' she asked as she opened the car door.

She may well have done - I'd been so absorbed looking at the Chomsky's that I couldn't be sure. 'Sounds like you were listening in,' I said slowly.

'Well, it's not a name I'm likely to forget, is it?' she said, running a paw through her red fur. I looked at her blankly.

'Never mind,' she said with a sigh, slapping me on the shoulder. 'See you tomorrow, Benji.'

Then I had it. 'Bouchard's? That was the Salon where -?' but by then she'd already gone, into the depot.

Later on, foregoing my usual evening drive and deciding to have an early night like a good little kitty should, I thought about Taki's words as she got out of the car, or rather the sadness with which she said them, and that slap on the shoulder. Both seemed to say the same thing: *You've got a long way to go, pal.*

The stuff between my ears wasn't just turning to jelly. It was practically dribbling out of my nostrils.

3.

The next morning I was up bright and early. After my initial restlessness I'd slept like a babe, and I felt good. The sun was shining and the sky was cloudless. For the first time in a long time, I felt ready for something.

Montcrieff Terrace was in the Lascelles district, and like half a dozen other streets I'd just driven through in the area, it was full of four storey faded brick buildings that you could imagine decades earlier being the exclusive playground for well-to-do business types. Only somewhere along the line they'd all moved out, and what had once been a haven for the extremely wealthy was now the kind of place you only ended up in if you had nowhere else to go. Even with the sun streaming down it looked shabby.

Parking up the car, I looked at the buildings more closely. Despite their size, I wondered whether anyone who'd lived round here even before The Terror would've had much space – presumably when the money still lived in the area, each building had been home to one family; but when it left it looked like all the properties had been divided up, resulting in a series of tiny business ventures squashed together at pavement level, among them a drugstore, a Fortune Teller's, something called Carrie's Collector's Emporium, a Butcher's, a tattoo parlour – all of them long since closed. As for the floors above the ground level premises, all but two looked deserted; my guess was that if anything did occupy those floors, they had more legs than the rest of us and lived in webs. Of all the businesses that had been on Montcrieff Terrace, only three appeared to remain; a crummy-looking bar at the entrance to the street called Kowalski's, the Salon at the far end, and, almost slap-bang between the two, looking in only slightly better condition than the bar, Chomsky's Pawnbroker's, its three faded golden balls hanging above the door. But of the three it was the Salon that caught the attention.

Sitting in its own space at the end of the terrace and blocking off the end of the road like something from an Ideal Homes Exhibition, Bouchard's Salon was the exact opposite of its neighbours – well-maintained, clean, and exclusive looking. The brickwork was perfect. Windows sparkled. Plush-looking curtains not faded by sunlight hung in the windows on all three floors. The roof and gutters looked like someone went up and cleaned them on a weekly basis. Even the doorknobs gleamed. The whole place reeked of perfection and new money. It also looked about as real as the plastic figures on top of a wedding cake.

The location didn't help – in a prosperous part of town, such a garish place would've looked okay if a little ostentatious; but here amongst such lowly companions, it stuck out like a sore thumb. In a strange way, it was the Salon that lowered the tone; the other places at least looked like they belonged here.

Turning back towards the Chomsky's, I was reminded of my initial reaction the day before – that this whole thing was probably just a neighbourly argument which had turned ugly: it was hard to imagine either side having anything in common. After a quick glance at the sign above the door – CHOMSKY'S PAWNBROKERS – FAMILY BUSINESS FOR OVER 50 YEARS – I pushed the doorknob on the wire-fronted door, and, a small bell above me announcing my presence, I stepped inside.

The whole place felt like an enormous Rabbit hutch, composed as it was of a series of locked cages and hatches, inside which various items of junk gathered dust on tables: an incomplete set of encyclopaedias, spines bleached almost colourless by sunlight; a grimy-looking box camera set next to a battered leather case; a classical guitar with two strings missing; tray after tray of undistinguished and unpolished jewellery. My guess was that when these objects were exchanged for money, their owners looked on it as an added bonus that they wouldn't be coming back for them. Between the cages a narrow walkway led to the counter, itself inside a cage, a large mesh grille cut into its front opening inwards on a hinge to allow for transactions, the counter littered with paper pushed through spikes. Making my way towards it, I watched pale sunlight as it strained its way through the metal hutches, illuminating the flecks of dust that hovered in the air like grey snowflakes. An aroma of barely-concealed despair accompanied me as I walked, along with the smell of soap.

'Mr Spriteman?'

Hearing the voice so close by, I jumped. Slightly behind me and to my right stood Sascha Chomsky, paws knitted together in front of her. 'My brother's in the back,' she told me. 'I'll take you through.' Unlocking another section of cage to the left of the counter led through to a doorway covered with a beaded curtain. Moving it aside I entered the room beyond, where Willie

Chomsky was sitting at a large table, in front of him a pile of cogs and springs.

'Get in there you goddamned son of a –' the little Dog muttered as he tried to slot something into the back of the clock he was holding, a piece of ash from the cigarette at the corner of his mouth falling onto the cogs.

'Willard,' Sascha said in a hushed voice, 'Mr Spriteman is here.'

'Yeah? You been to see her yet?' he said, not taking his eye off the clock while his cigarette burned off some of the dust in the room, 'Miss Boo-shard?'

'Uh, I thought it best to get the full story from you first,' I told him.

'Fair enough,' he said, stubbing what was left of the cigarette into an ashtray. 'We can talk out front – I need a break from that damned clock anyway.' Following him out, we went back into the shop.

'Okay,' he began. 'It really got started about a month ago. Before that, it was no big shakes: we didn't like her and she didn't like us. She looked down her nose at us, you know.'

'She thinks she's one of the elite,' Sascha put in.

'Damn right she does. But she's no better than the rest of us. Acts like butter wouldn't melt when she has customers around, but when they leave – oh boy, does she change.'

'Yeah?' I said, remembering what Taki had told me. 'How?'

'How? She shrieks like a lunatic is how. The noise is unbelievable. I don't know what she pays those girls but I'd say they earn it, having to put up with that. Half of 'em come running out in tears.'

'And there's a lot of them,' Sascha said. 'Some of them don't stay very long.'

'Anyway, we put up with it as long as we could,'

Chomsky continued, 'but one day she started up again worse than ever, so we waited until it'd quietened down again and decided to have it out with her. We'd just got to the door when it started again, even louder.'

'Wait a second,' I interrupted. 'You must be twenty, thirty yards from her place. You can hear this going on from that distance?'

The Chomsky's nodded. 'And that day was particularly bad,' Chomsky said. 'It sounded like murder being committed. So we waited for a break in the noise *again* then I shouted through the door and told her to zip it or else I'd get the cops down.'

'And that's when she came to us,' Sascha said.

'Yeah – at seven o'clock the next morning!' Chomsky continued. 'Squawking away outside the front door about the condition of our shop. When I finally got the door open I thought she might stop for a second, but oh no, she just carried on. And that's when –'

Next to him, Sascha began to whimper.

'Hey, shush now,' Chomsky said, putting his arm around her shoulder and patting it before continuing. 'That's when Gino came running through from the back room, barking. He usually did when he heard a different voice, but when he *saw* her, he went crazy – he was so loud that he even managed to drown her out! When she realised we couldn't hear her, she stomped off.'

'I don't think she was used to anyone talking over her, especially an Old Dog,' Sascha added.

'And that kind of led to the business with the sign.' As Chomsky spoke, he kept his leaky eye on a customer who'd just entered the shop.

'While she'd been shooting her mouth off she had a go at our sign. Well, once we'd both calmed down a bit we decided she was right about that. It does look a bit tatty, and we had a little money set aside, so –'

'– we got a new one,' Sascha finished.

'It was a good 'un too,' Chomsky said proudly, 'written in big letters, nice and classy. Then the morning after the sign was put up I went outside to look at it and it'd been defaced. And I don't need to tell you by *who*.'

'We've kept it as evidence,' Sascha said. 'Show him, Willard.'

'Damn right I'll show him,' Chomsky muttered, scurrying off into a dark corner of the room. When he came back, it was with a large wooden board in his arms. 'There,' he said, holding it aloft, 'how do you like *them* apples?'

It was certainly striking. The original lettering was laid out in three rows – presumably a row each for their names – and written in a bright yellow typeface. Unfortunately, the only things still in yellow now were the letters *W, S* and *C* at the start of each row, the remaining lettering redone in thick black paint so it now said something completely different.

'"We Sell Crap"!' Chomsky shouted, pointing a nicotine-stained claw unnecessarily at the defaced surface. 'Goddamned sons of bitches. The things is, the sign writer won't take it back, so we've had to put the old sign back up. If it wasn't for the – hey, are you okay?'

Getting my paw up to my face in time, I was able to pass my laughter off as a coughing fit. Then suddenly his expression changed to one of fury. 'Hey!' he yelled, dropping the sign on the floor and marching past me towards the customer who'd come in earlier. 'Get your mitts off that, you morbid bastard – it ain't for sale.' Startled, the Terrier headed for the door. 'And make sure you tell everyone else too!' Chomsky called out as he left. 'If I want to look at an asshole in my shop I'll become a contortionist.'

After swearing a few more times he came back over to me. 'You okay now?' he asked, stopping briefly on the way to look at something I couldn't see.

'Something went down the wrong way, that's all,' I told him, clearing my throat a few times. 'Um, going back to the sign; so you didn't actually *see* her d –'

'No, but who else could it have been? And then, not long after that the letter arrived. I've got it here somewhere –' rooting around in his pants' pocket, Chomsky eventually produced a sheet of crumpled paper. Smoothing it out, he cleared his throat. 'Here, listen to this: *"Dear Mr Chomsky, I am contacting you following a distressing communication I received today from my client, Ms Mimi Bouchard of Montcrieff Terrace, who was looking for advice with regard to your continued campaign of harassment and threats against her, culminating in a near attack on my client a few mornings ago by a member of your household, which left my client fearful not only for her personal safety but that of her clientele should a similar incident take place away from the environs of your property. After giving the matter some thought, and, in my capacity as senior partner of Wareham, Krukowski & Yang, I advised Ms Bouchard to apply for a restraining order, preventing you or any member of your family from entering the private space of Ms Bouchard's property to a distance of 25 yards, and from contacting her or any of her employees or customers. Finally, I would say in closing that it was with some regret that I suggested these measures, but with a vested interest in proceedings with regard to the property, I felt that this was the correct action to take. Sincerely yours, Donny Wareham, Senior Partner, on behalf of Wareham, Krukowski & Yang Property Management."* Horseshit,' Chomsky concluded, passing me the letter. 'Absolute horseshit.'

Frowning, I looked at it closely. Although it was typed on official-looking headed paper and contained the obligatory scrawled signature on the bottom, it felt wrong, like a cheap scare tactic. 'What did you do when you got this?' I asked, handing the letter back.

'Do?' Chomsky said. 'Nothing. It's a joke, right? That stuff about not going over to her property? Apart from that once we've never been anywhere near it. And as for the "near attack", if she hadn't come to us that never would've happened. Not that Gino *would* have attacked her anyway – he was just noisy, that's all. Always was. Admittedly, he got worse after The Terror, but –'

'I don't think Gino liked the fact that we changed and he hadn't,' Sascha said. 'You know – into what we are now. I think he was jealous of us. And that's why he barked so much.'

'Okay...' I said, trying to think of an appropriate response. But maybe she was right – sometimes, looking at animals that hadn't changed you couldn't help thinking, *why me and not you?* It was a strange sensation. But jealous or not, there was something rather touching about the fact that they saw themselves as a family, despite not even all being the same species, let alone the same breeds.

'Well, even if he *did* bark a lot, he didn't deserve what happened next,' Chomsky said.

I asked him to tell me what happened.

'A couple of nights later we decided to go out for a walk,' he said, his voice hushed. 'We were going to take Gino but he'd taken himself off to his kennel in the back yard, so we went without him. We'd been out for about forty-five minutes when it started to get chilly, so we came back. It was dark by then. Normally, when he heard someone approaching in the alley he barked the place down. Only this time he didn't. So Sascha went over to his kennel to see what was wrong.'

'And I – trod in a puddle,' she said, her voice wavering. 'But it hadn't been raining.'

'We only realised it was blood when I flicked my lighter on,' Chomsky said. 'Somehow, I managed to get him out of the kennel. And then I saw the bullet hole in his skull.' Emitting a small strangled sob, Sascha went into the back room.

'Did anybody see anything?' I asked.

'Not a thing. But besides us there's only Sadie lives around here. She heard the shot, though.'

'Sadie?'

'Our neighbour,' he said. 'Goat, lives a few doors along. Eventually the cops turned up and had a look around, but it was pretty obvious they weren't expecting to find who did it.'

'But they did treat it as a crime scene?'

'They asked questions if that's what you mean. Said it was probably kids – even after they'd eventually spoken to *her*.' He pointed a claw in the Salon's general direction. 'I know there are some punks out there, but to do that – have a look for yourself.'

Following him through the network of cages, he led me over to the spot he'd stopped at earlier after chasing the customer out of the shop. In a small nook between the cages sat a large, rough-coated Collie with a thick black coat, a long black and brown snout and a beautiful white ruff of fur at its neck. Dead glass eyes stared off into the distance.

'That's where we were going last night after we left you – to pick him up from the taxidermists,' Chomsky said. 'Looks good, huh? They've done the best they could with –' pointing to a spot just above the Dog's ear, the stitches were partially covered by fur. 'It ain't perfect, but under the circumstances… nah – I don't think kids would've done *that*.'

Unnerved by the Dog at our feet, I manoeuvred Chomsky back towards the counter, asking questions as I did so. 'You mentioned someone called Butler yesterday,' I said, the glass eyes now thankfully out of sight.

He gave me a funny look. 'Butler? Oh, wait a minute – not someone *called* Butler. Madam, down the road there? She *has* a Butler – an old mutt called Moseley – gold teeth, peaked cap, the whole bit; vicious old bastard. Lives up in that mansion of hers out of town. My money's on him for shooting Gino. On her instructions of course.'

'Why?'

'Gut feeling. I saw him outside once, chasing an Old Rat along the street with a broom. Looked to me like he was enjoying himself too much. And the day before Gino was shot I spotted him hanging around in the alley. But as soon as he saw me he moved away.'

'Presumably you told the police this.'

'Sure I did. But they'd already decided it was kids.' He shook his head sadly. 'The thing I don't understand is why she stays around here at all. With the kind of money she has, she could go anywhere.'

When I left a few minutes later, I found the same question was puzzling me too.

4.

Heading over to Bouchard's Salon, I was once again impressed by how pristine it looked, how *exclusive*. Was it possible to make so much money from cutting animal fur that you could afford a mansion and a butler? Perhaps she'd inherited. I decided against it – in my experience, the kind of animals born into money usually went out and spent it, and didn't plough it into business.

Turning the shiny doorknob, I stepped inside. Above me, a crisp bell sounded. And before I had the door closed, I rocked on my heels as the odours of the place assaulted me.

I can't pretend I know what the average beauty parlour smelled like in Sappy times, but my guess was that even the most pungent ones had nothing on this. First, it was the sharp, alcoholic whiff of nail polish jabbing its talons up my nose and into my brain, closely followed by wave upon wave of tangy shampoos and sickly cloying perfumes, the latter pumped into the air from oddly-shaped bottles. On their own these smells were bad enough; but when they were applied to the wet fur of the clientele, it made the air practically toxic. The worst of the stench came from an immense, elderly Guinea Pig – not the best smelling of creatures to begin with – who was seated beneath a dryer reading a magazine as she tucked into a large bag of sunflower seeds on her lap. And while I can't claim to know exactly what barbequing geriatric livestock in a hayloft *would* smell like, I imagine it would be pretty close to the stink coming from under that dryer.

As I wiped the tears away from my eyes with a handkerchief, a sharp voice asked, 'Can I help you?'

In front of me stood a standoffish looking Balinese with ash-grey fur, wearing a tight red sweater and a pair of large black spectacles, behind which were a pair of pale, ice-blue eyes. 'I'd like to speak with Miss Bouchard,' I told her.

'I see,' she said without emotion. 'I'm afraid she's not here. Perhaps you could call back another day.'

'Or I could call on her at home if she's there. It's rather important.' I smiled but her expression didn't budge.

'Wait here. I'll see if I can contact her.' With that, she vanished behind a curtain at the back of the room.

With my eyes and nose as used to their surroundings as they were ever going to be, I started to look around. A few of the clientele watched me as I did, but the staff just carried on with their work. The main feature of the place of course were the giant mirrors, the walls behind them painted a deep maroon and finished with black edging. Looking carefully at each mirror in turn, I couldn't see a single smear or paw-mark on any of them. In spaces between some of the mirrors were hung what looked like photographs, but were in fact framed pictures taken from newspapers and magazines, complete with captions: Ms Bouchard with Mayor Perryman at the opening of a soup kitchen on Belmont Ave; Ms Bouchard chairing the inaugural meeting of the Loggia Foundation, looking into the causes of poverty;

Ms Bouchard, owner of the Bouchard Salon dancing with an admirer at a charity dinner to raise funds for the cities' homeless. And at the centre of every picture showing all her teeth for the camera, a delicate-looking black Cat with a small, heart-shaped face.

Following the pictures in turn, I was now quite close to the curtain the Balinese had disappeared through, and when she returned she seemed surprised to find that I'd moved. 'I've spoken to Ms Bouchard,' she said, blinking, 'and she says she can see you at her home at two o'clock. If you're late however, you won't be allowed admittance. She's very busy.' Handing me a business card for the Salon she added, 'The address is on the back.'

'Your employer seems to move in influential circles,' I said, nodding at the walls as I slipped the card into my pocket. She didn't reply.

'Well, thank you for your help, Miss –'

'Vincent,' she answered reluctantly. 'Caro Vincent.'

'Miss Vincent,' I said, tipping my hat.

Back outside and again able to breathe, I checked the address on the back of the overly-designed business card. It seemed that Miss Bouchard's 'Mansion' was quite a way out of town, but it was still only eleven o'clock so I had a fair bit of time to kill first. Walking away from the Salon I headed back up the street and took a right, into an alleyway at the rear of the main buildings.

If the street entrances looked a bit grim, the back ones were truly dismal. Cleared of garbage, I daresay the alley was pretty wide; but thanks to the masses of boxes, crates and overflowing trashcans, most of it was single file only. To the left, a series of broken down fences just about kept the overgrown gardens of the empty properties from also spilling out into the alley.

Having said that, the Chomsky's backyard wasn't half bad, with the exception of a few weeds poking through the flagstones. Opening the gate, I went in and had a look at Gino's kennel, over in the corner. The area around it had been vigorously scrubbed, presumably to get rid of the bloodstains. Crouching, I looked inside the kennel. There was nothing to see, but the smell of Dog lingered. Standing back up I saw that I was being watched, Sascha Chomsky eyeing me behind the net curtain. With a slight nod I moved away, out of the yard.

A cursory glance through what remained of the next few fences only revealed more plant life. Then I came to a fence in better condition about half the height of the others, on the other side of which was a lawn full of half-chewed grass.

Opening the gate, I headed up the path to the slightly open back door and knocked.

'Help you?' a muffled voice called out beyond the door.

'Hope so. I'm looking for Sadie.'

'That's me,' the muffled voice replied. 'Give me a second.'

I did so, and watched a black hoof appear round the side of the door and pull it inwards even further, so that a pair of wide-spaced eyes could peer up at me through the gap.

'Benji Spriteman,' I said, lowering my license towards them. 'I'm looking into the death of Gino Chomsky.'

'I guess you'd better come inside.' Hooking her hoof round the door once more, she opened it wide enough for me to enter.

'Take a seat.'

As I did she turned to face me, her back to the door. Lifting one of her hind legs, she pushed it over until it was almost closed, her hoof adding another print to the countless others covering the bottom third of the kitchen door.

I liked Goats. I liked the fact that they didn't care.

When The Terror changed what seemed to be the vast majority of us a few years earlier, it soon became apparent that not everyone had changed in the same way. For most of us, it meant that as well as the ability to speak Human languages, our backs straightened out and we began to walk on two legs instead of four. But for some animals the change wasn't physical, and these animals remained on four legs, the difference being that now you could have a conversation with them if you – and they – were so inclined. Most of these creatures – livestock, for example – accepted their lot and carried on pretty much as before. But for some, the changes brought differing fortunes. To Horses, this new form of existence was nothing but frustrating – as before, they had looks, grace and speed on their side; but unfortunately they were too big to live anywhere except in stables; whereas Goats, despite still being as ugly as sin, could now live pretty much anywhere they liked as long as they weren't too fat to squeeze through a doorframe.

'This place used to be a pet shop, if you're wondering about the smell,' this one said as she moved away from the door. 'Pre-Terror, that is. But when all the animals changed they couldn't get away quick enough.'

'You didn't think to join them?'

'No, I had it cushy compared to most of them – I lived out there in the garden. I was the store's top draw back then. Didn't much care for the winters though. So when everyone left –'

'You came inside.'

'I don't need much help. As long as Sascha comes

along and plants some grass seed for me every once in a while, I'm good. How is she?'

'I'd say up and down. Mostly down. What happened that night?'

'I was in the front room, and I fell asleep reading the paper Sascha brought round.' I was still trying to imagine how Goats could read anything with their eyes so far apart when she said, 'Anyway, I woke up cold, because the back door was open.'

'You leave your door open?'

'Most of the time. Just a few inches. I lock it at night of course, but it's a nuisance to be messing with it all day. Opening it's easy enough – jump up, kick the bolt loose – no problem. But locking it, you have to make sure the bolt's in the right place so it slots into the groove when you kick it. Anyhow, I came in here to close it for the night and heard Gino making a terrible racket outside.'

'Even worse than usual?'

She nodded. 'Usually it was just barking, but this was snarling too. I'd decided I was going to go take a look when I heard a sharp, cracking sound and Gino stopped making his noise. I didn't think for a second that it might be gunfire. I was just glad that he'd stopped yapping. And after that I locked my door.'

'You didn't hear anything afterwards?'

'No. Place was as quiet as a graveyard. Until Sascha knocked at the door.'

'Would you say killing Gino is the kind of thing Miss Bouchard would be capable of?'

'I'd say it's the kind of thing she'd get someone else to do for her, if that temper of hers is anything to go by – she screeches like a stuck Owl at the girls in that Salon. But I don't think she'd get her own paws dirty.'

'You've never had any trouble with her yourself?'

'I'd be surprised if she even knew I existed – I rarely go any further than the back yard. And with fur like this, I'm a long way past needing a shampoo and set.'

I'd just started to laugh when there was a loud crash outside. Getting out of my seat, I just managed to catch a glimpse of a prematurely balding Mastiff with slightly bulging eyes at the window before it darted out of sight.

Feeling a tug at the leg of my pants, I looked down. Sadie stared up at me quizzically. Raising a claw to my mouth, I made a gesture for her to move back. Inching the door open, I eased myself through the gap as quietly as I could. The noise had been caused by the trashcan the Mastiff had knocked over, leaving the pathway covered in garbage. As I looked at it, I heard the muffled sound of a car door slamming, presumably round at the front of the street. Deciding I didn't have time to get there before it drove off, I hurried back into Sadie's kitchen.

'You expecting visitors?' I asked her.

'No. You don't think this is to do with –'

'Maybe.' Rushing through the far door into what I hoped was Sadie's living room, I made for the window but saw nothing, just heard the car zooming off into the distance.

I turned to find Sadie looking up at me from the doorway. 'Any Mastiffs live around here?'

She shook her head. 'Not that I know of. But I'll keep my eye out for 'em now.'

'It might be an idea,' I said. Asking a few more questions, I cleaned up the trash outside and left.

Out in the alley, I had a quick root around to see if our friend had dropped anything, but found zip. Back on the street, I wondered whether maybe it was worth going to the Salon again, ask if they knew anything about what'd just happened; but somehow I doubted that I'd get a satisfactory answer.

Instead I went back to the Pawnbrokers. Hearing the bell above the door, the Chomsky's blinked at me from the counter. 'I don't suppose you saw the car that just sped by?'

They looked at each other. 'No. We can't see much of the street from back here.'

'It was being driven by a Mastiff. Ever seen one in the area?'

'Pop-eyed and ugly? Yeah, I've seen him – goes in to the Salon from time to time. Why?'

'Just wondering.' Before they could ask me anything more, I left.

Maybe he'd been in the Salon when I visited earlier; it certainly seemed possible. I could ask Ms Bouchard about him later. I could also ask her if there was anything specifically she didn't like about the Chomsky's, or if they'd done something to upset her that they hadn't told me about, because although they seemed nice enough, there was something about the pair of them that made me a little wary. A little digging might be in order; and I knew just the creature to do it.

Hungry, I headed over to the only place in the street I hadn't been to – Kowalski's bar. And, while I marvelled that there really were Kowalski's out there who weren't in the police force, I ordered a tuna oil on the rocks and a steak sandwich from the mutt himself while he wiped his paws on his greasy bib. Asking if there was a phone I could use, he pointed over towards the washrooms where I eventually picked out a murky-looking booth near the entrance. Stepping inside, I dialled in the semi-darkness.

'Eth?' a voice whispered in my ear.

'It's me, Harvey.' I said. 'Take your teeth out.'

'O. An on a thek –' Anticipating the usual wet sucking noise followed by what sounded like two large candles being dropped onto a table, I moved the phone away from my ear. Hearing a voice totally unlike the first one begin to speak, I moved it back again. 'Hi, Benji,' it said. 'What's up?'

'I need you to find out anything you can on a Mimi Bouchard, proprietor of the Salon on Montcrieff Terrace,' I said, lowering my voice a touch. 'Also, anything on a couple called the Chomsky's who run the Pawnbroker's on the same street.'

'Will do,' he said cheerfully. 'I'll be in your area tomorrow, actually. Want me to bring anything I find out along to your office?'

'Sure,' I said. 'You or Laurence.'

Laughing, he hung up.

Back at the bar, Kowalski was polishing a glass in his paw. The glass squeaked.

'Quiet round here,' I said. He shrugged. 'After all the fuss, I mean.'

'What fuss?' he grunted, clumping the glass down on the bar.

'I heard there was a shooting.'

'Oh, that. Yeah, an Old Dog got popped.'

'Strange that,' I mused. 'I mean, why would anyone want to kill an *Old* Dog?'

'Beats me. I'll go see if your sandwich is ready.'

For maybe a minute, I stared at the glass on the bar that'd just been cleaned. It was still dirty. Finally Kowalski appeared with a plate.

'Your sandwich,' he said, dropping it in front of me. 'Enjoy.'

A few bites later I wondered if he was being sarcastic. After wrestling with the steak for five minutes, I gave up. Not long after he came back, he looked at all the bits on my plate and gave another shrug. 'Anything else?' he asked.

'Yeah,' I said. 'A doggy bag.'

He blinked at me. 'A doggy bag?'

'Yeah. I want to take all those stringy bits of meat home and knit them into a vest.'

Muttering to himself he started to move away, taking the plate with him. 'One last thing,' I said.

He stopped, his back to me. 'What?'

'The Salon down at the bottom of the road there. Ever had any trouble with the owner?'

Turning, he cast his gaze around the bar. 'Somehow I don't think this place would be quite her scene,' he said before shuffling off into the back.

Out on the street I looked at my watch. It was now lunchtime. After heading somewhere a bit more salubrious to grab a coffee and a Danish, I decided to make an early start and head across town to the Bouchard residence, so I'd get there in time; heaven forbid that I shouldn't be 'allowed admittance'. Normally, such a command would've resulted in me arriving late on purpose – but for some reason, this time I didn't think that would be the right thing to do.

If Ms Bouchard insisted on me being there on time, I would be.

5.

In the end it was a good thing I had set off early, as I pulled up outside the Bouchard residence with only five minutes to spare.

To say the place was out in the sticks was putting it mildly. On leaving the city, I was fairly convinced I was heading in the right direction for the first half hour or so. But after entering a dense forest and navigating a series of hairpin bends, I started to wonder. When the foliage became so thick the daylight was dimmed to a murky green, I switched on my lights. This did little to brighten things up, but it meant I could spot a few Squirrels in the trees and the odd Rabbit eyeing me carefully along the sides of the road. I guessed that most of them weren't Olds, because I hadn't seen anything that had been run over. I made a note that on my way back – if I ever got there in the first place – I'd stop and try and talk to a few of them; if I got the response I was expecting to get from Ms Bouchard, they at least might be able to tell me something.

Twenty or so hairpin bends later, I was on the point of giving up when suddenly the trees thinned a bit and daylight returned. Seconds later I was pulling up and switching off my lights, and looking at two floors of ugly but no doubt expensive real estate from the wrong side of a pair of freshly-painted black gates.

Whilst undoubtedly impressive, the Bouchard residence could hardly be described as a mansion, and I wondered if Chomsky had actually been up here or had just made a general assumption about the place. Getting out of the car, I stood at the gates and looked through its bars at the grounds. The grass was a bright, liquid green and covered an area about the size of a football pitch, and looked like it was trimmed with geometric precision. Running through the centre of it, a long gravel path led to a small flight of creamy-marble steps and the house itself. Between the gates and the house on the left was what looked like an ornamental Fishpond, and around that were some very expensive-looking stone pots full of bright red flowers. With nobody else in sight I called out to the inhabitants of the pond, but didn't expect a reply – chances were the Fish living there would be Olds, and if they weren't Olds chances were they'd be too posh to talk to the likes of me.

Turning back to the gates I looked for a buzzer, but buzzer there was none. It was now almost three minutes to two; and with no other options, it looked like I was going to have to resort to undignified measures. Readying my fist above the horn on the car's steering wheel, my chance for fun was stopped when the door of the house opened and a smallish figure in a black suit appeared and took his sweet time walking down the drive towards me. When he was close enough, I caught a momentary glint of brightness from his mouth: a gold tooth. Unless someone else in Ms Bouchard's employ also had gold fillings, I was looking at Moseley. With any luck I'd get to quiz him on the way out; if I wanted to make my appointment, I didn't have time to do it now.

'Help you?' he said in the gruffest, least helpful voice imaginable.

'I have an appointment with the lady of the house,' I said, eventually finding his eyes under the peak of his cap. 'I was told to be here by two o'clock sharp or go home. So here I am, with a minute or two to spare.'

For a few seconds he looked at me like he hadn't understood a word I'd said. He was an elderly Boxer with a leathery face and a jutting chin, and his small, beady bespectacled brown eyes never blinked as he watched me. They say you shouldn't judge someone on first appearances, but with this one it was hard not to – he looked and smelled like trouble. Whether he killed Gino or not remained to be seen.

'You appear to be staring at me,' he growled.

'I thought it might make you open the gates a little quicker,' I replied, keeping my face cheerful.

He didn't like that; the heavy jaw dropped open momentarily before closing again. Dragging a ring of keys the size of a fist from one of his pockets, he slowly moved forward and opened the gates. Turning from me, he shuffled out of the way, muttering to himself as he did so.

'Say something, gramps?' I asked.

When he turned back it wasn't quite as slowly. 'I can close this gate again as I easily as I opened it, you know,' he said, heavy jaw jutting forward.

'I'm sure you could,' I replied. 'But at the speed you go at I could have robbed the family silver and be back out before then.'

In reply the old mutt spat into the grass before making his way back towards the house.

Driving past him, I parked up in front of the steps and got out of the car. Behind me, the old coot was still taking his time so I decided to speed him up a bit.

Stepping up to the door, I grabbed hold of the knocker and banged it so hard that the whole door shook.

It had the desired effect. 'Hey!' he yelled out, suddenly breaking into a trot and stomping up the steps towards me. 'You wait for *me*! Understand? You wait for *me*.' His eyes blazed up at me from under his cap. It was all I could do to stop myself asking for his opinion on dead Dogs. Instead, I made a big show of checking my watch and made a few clucking noises with my tongue. Barging past me, he started muttering to himself again as he opened the door. I followed him in.

Inside, the hall was as plush as I'd imagined. It was decked out in wood panelling, and had a large carpet in the centre of the parquet floor that looked like it'd never been stepped on. Ahead, a highly-polished mahogany staircase twisted upwards. Besides Moseley's heavy, deliberate steps there was nothing to hear. Turning, he stared right at me. *Follow me,* his beady little eyes said. *No funny business.*

Instead of leading me upstairs he went right, down a corridor lined with vases full of alien-looking flowers, the stink of which nearly choked me. At the end of the corridor he stopped before a heavy, varnished door and knocked at it, listening intently. A few seconds later, he grasped the door handle and opened the door slowly over a thick carpet. Moving to one side, he showed me the flat of his leathery paw, indicating that I was to go in. I'd barely crossed the threshold into the dimly-lit room when he closed the door behind me.

'*Yes?*' a surprised-sounding voice said from the other side of the room.

'Ms Bouchard? My name's Spriteman. I spoke to a colleague of yours earlier today – Miss Vincent. She arranged a –'

'Oh yes, of course. And it's *Mimi*, please – let's not

stand on ceremony. And do sit down. Would you care for a drink? It's such a trek up here, I know.'

'Not for me, thanks.'

'Or me. Which means we can get straight down to business.'

It wasn't until this last sentence that I managed to locate her, reclining on a light charcoal velvet loveseat which was almost the same colour as her fur and the trouser suit she was wearing. If it hadn't been for the abundance of jewellery she wore and the brightness of her eyes – a luminescent orangey-brown – it would've taken me even longer.

To see a Chartreaux anywhere is rare, but imagining one on Montcrieff Terrace almost seemed ridiculous, even within the confines of the Salon. She was small and delicate looking, with short, blue-grey fur and had a nose that looked like a small button of soft, wet liquorice. Her whiskers were incredibly fine, and not a fur was out of place. She sat with her legs loosely crossed, her paws nestled amongst the cushions around her. During the whole time I was there, I don't think I saw her blink.

'So then, Mr...Spriteman,' she rolled the word around her mouth like the finest champagne before spitting it out. 'How much do you want?'

'Pardon me?'

'And there was me thinking you were different,' she said, looking off to one side of the room. 'I'm getting down to business, Mr Spriteman.'

Either she was offering me hush money or our wires were crossed. Before I had a chance to reply she continued.

'I offer help to all kinds of organisations, big and small, and I'm glad to do so. But my time is precious. So: how much do you want? I won't ask you again.'

'Ms Bouchard, I'm not here looking for money. I –'

'*Not* looking for money? Then why are you here?'

'To discuss the situation with the Chomsky's, your neighbours on Montcrieff Terrace. I wanted to ask you about –'

She looked like she'd been slapped in the face. 'Do you have any identification?'

'Sure.' I showed her my license.

She looked at it in disbelief. '*A Private Detective?*'

'Like I said, I want to talk to you about your dispute with the Chomsky's. As you know, somebody shot their brother recently, and not surprisingly they're none too happy about it.'

For maybe ten seconds' words seemed to fail her. Then she recovered and gave me a few dozen fairly quickly. 'You... you want to talk about – did you just call them my *neighbours?* They're not my neighbours – even if they almost do live in my lap in that hovel of theirs. But you're saying you've come all this way to talk about these *creatures* with me, and that yapping mutt of theirs?'

'It isn't yapping anymore, Ms Bouchard. Someone shot it in the head, remember?'

She gave me a look that could've frozen fire. As she gave it, I thought I heard a small ripping sound somewhere close to her but I saw nothing. Then she gave a little girlish chuckle and appeared to be in control again.

'And you think I have nothing better to do than...' she shook her head, smiling sweetly. 'Oh, Mr Sp –'

'I was thinking more about the old guy who showed me in here,' I interrupted. 'Just something I heard, you understand.'

'Oh, Mr Spriteman,' she continued, still smiling. 'Do you honestly think I would go to all that trouble to kill a Dog who barked too much? I find that very sad. Very sad indeed.'

'I thought about that myself, and it made me wonder if there was some other reason you disliked them so much. I saw the letter you sent them.'

'It's true I'd rather they weren't there, but I didn't kill their Dog. And the police don't seem to think I had anything to do with it. They said they didn't know who was responsible.' She cranked the smile up a notch. 'Tell me, Mr Spriteman – do you often work for free?'

I frowned at her.

'I only ask because my "neighbours" don't strike me as having a great deal of money – unless they *enjoy* living like that, of course – and I just wondered how on earth they were going to pay you for your...efforts.'

It had been at the back of my mind too. Batting it aside I said, 'You obviously don't have that problem – money, I mean. Maybe *you* should leave if you hate them so much – unless *you* enjoy slumming it down there on Montcrieff Terrace.'

The smile became so brittle I thought her lips might shatter. 'I think, Mr Spriteman, you've just asked your last question.' Tugging on a cord beside the loveseat, she didn't take her eyes off me. Nor me her – I'd become pretty good at staring animals down, and if she wanted a contest she could have one. We'd hardly been at it a minute when her expression changed and she looked away. *Moseley hasn't answered her call and she's wondering why.*

I stared on for maybe another ten, fifteen seconds or so and then rose. 'Looks like we've both been stood up,' I said, watching her squirm. 'A shame when the servant lets you down. Or so I imagine. I'll let myself out.' Turning my back on her I heard that ripping noise again, this time much louder. Looking back, I was just in time to see one of her paws vanish beneath the cushions; the top one now had a gash in it wide enough to fit a pocketbook inside.

'Something for the maid to do,' I said as stuffing spilled from the hole. 'Hope she has plenty of thread.' Raising my hat a fraction, I left.

Out in the corridor I realised that I hadn't had the chance to ask her half the questions I'd wanted, including about the identity of the Mastiff, but now I found I was more interested in Moseley. Strange, that he hadn't showed up like that. So I decided I'd try and find him.

As it had been when I arrived the house was eerily quiet, so I was able to wander about uninterrupted. The kitchen, laundry room and the few other places I looked in were unlocked and empty. Then, just as I was about to try upstairs, I spotted a door next to the staircase. It too was unlocked. A short flight of steps took me down to another door, but this one was locked. Crouching at the keyhole in the confined space, I could see nothing except the key in the lock on the other side of the door. Holding my breath, I waited and listened for a while but heard nothing; if it was Moseley on the other side of the door, he was waiting for me to leave.

As quietly as I could, I crept back up the stairs and headed outside to look for another possible way in, but didn't find one. As I looked, I noticed a rather scruffy creature of indeterminate species working in the garden. Calling out to them got no response, so I went over.

A few feet away, I called out once more, but again nothing. For a moment I thought about tapping them on the shoulder, but I didn't like the way they were wielding the spade. So I walked around in front of them and waved my paws around.

After a few seconds of this they saw me, and slowly

lowered the spade. Then even more slowly, they looked up at me.

He was a ragged Tom with badly-matted fur and chaotic, watery eyes. 'I'm looking for the butler,' I told him. 'Moseley. I need to speak to him.'

The Cat didn't even make an attempt at a reply. Instead he just looked vaguely in my direction with his barely-focused eyes. As the seconds ticked by I couldn't figure out whether the lights weren't on or he was putting on an act. Whichever it was he soon lost interest in me, and turned his attention back to the soil.

Deciding that trying again would be pointless, I walked away, suddenly wanting to be gone from this strange place.

Heading back towards the front of the house, the silence was disturbed by what sounded like a very noisy car coming up the long drive. By the time I'd reached the gravel path, the car was close enough for me to see its driver: a prematurely balding Mastiff with slightly bulging eyes, which bulged even further when they saw me. Without reducing speed, the Mastiff turned his steering wheel violently, sending the car into an ear-piercing spin, churning up first the gravel then the grass as it roared back down towards the gate.

Sprinting to my car, I climbed in and gunned the engine, yanked the steering wheel hard to my right and pressed down hard on the gas. As the house shrunk into the distance behind me, I looked in my rear view mirror. Back in the garden, the Cat with the chaotic eyes was still working with his shovel, back turned towards me.

6.

I caught up with the Mastiff pretty much straight away. Evidently not the brightest creature in town, he'd decided that the best thing to do was get out of his car and shut the gates after him, but hadn't even got as far as closing one of them when he looked up and saw me speeding towards him. As I pressed down a little harder on the accelerator, he abandoned the gate and jumped back into his car.

With the momentum on my side, any advantage he had was short lived. By the time we were in among the trees, I was close enough to see the back of his head in his rear windscreen; a second later, I was close enough to see his bulging eyes staring at me in his rear-view mirror. I was still looking at them when he flicked his lights on. Turning my attention back to the road, I saw it cut away sharply to the left. Too late to take the turn, I stamped on the brakes just in time to stop the car from ploughing into a tree. By the time I'd got my breath back and turned on my lights, I could just make out the taillights of the Mastiff's car through the trees as it negotiated its way through the twists and turns of the road ahead.

After backing up and taking the left turn, I drove as

quickly as I dared in an attempt to catch up, only reducing my speed slightly on a couple of bad bends, my lights flashing crazy patterns across the tree trunks. Catching sight of his taillights once more through a gap in the foliage and seeing tracks ahead in the dim light, I gritted my teeth and turned the wheel at them before realising that instead of a turn in the road I was in fact speeding towards a set of skid marks where another driver had misjudged a bend. Three trees loomed up before me in a row; aiming for what I judged was the biggest gap between them, I shot towards it and hoped for the best. To my immense relief, the gap was bigger than I thought; not only did the car get through, but so did most of the paintwork. Even better, once I'd gulped my heart back down into my chest, I realised that my little detour had cut the bend out altogether, saving me a few seconds; and, with a straight downward slope ahead of me, I felt sure that when I got to the bottom and took the next bend, I'd be right on his tail.

But when I did he wasn't there.

After cursing myself, the car, the forest and anything else I could think of, I eased off the gas, sure that I'd lost him. Slowing to a pace that wouldn't actually kill me, I let off a couple more curses to make me feel better. By the time I took the next bend I was just starting to enjoy myself. Then I noticed something strange happening up ahead.

For some reason, the trees were raining branches.

Easing off the gas a bit more, I wondered what the hell was going on. Ahead of me, the road was pretty much impassable, covered by a thick carpet of leaves and wooden limbs dropping from the trees on both sides of the road. And in the midst of this blizzard of falling branches was a car moving slowly forwards as bits of tree bounced off its bodywork.

It seemed I'd caught up with the Mastiff again after all.

Getting as close to this bizarre scene as I dared, I watched as what appeared to be half a tree landed on the Mastiff's roof with a loud boom before sliding onto the ground. As it fell, something resembling a large divot of moss splatted against his nearside window, quickly followed by a second one on the opposite side of the vehicle, which in turn was followed by a volley of pellets pinging against the side of the car, denting the metal. They'd barely stopped when a fresh round started, aimed slightly higher up, peppering the side windows and cracking the glass. Then, another large branch thudded down onto the roof of the car but didn't bounce off. And suddenly there were enough gaps in the branches for me to see who was responsible for this destruction.

Squirrels.

Spotting one, I saw them everywhere, not just in the trees. And they weren't the cute little Old ones you saw in the park either, but at least twice that size; hundreds of them, on the ground, peering around tree trunks or high up in the branches, gnawing and breaking off the smaller branches around them and hurling them at the car below, their eyes little black balls of hatred.

Hearing breaking glass, I looked back at the car. A small hole had appeared in the Mastiff's back window, the glass around it resembling a large oblong of cracked ice. The car's engine revved crazily but the vehicle barely moved, immobilised by the carpet of debris, its roar matched by the high-pitched cheering from the side of the road. But the cheering didn't last long as once again the Squirrels took up arms, scores of them up on their haunches, armed with slingshots firing mud or stones, some using blowpipes made from hollowed-out branches spitting out acorns, others still without weapons throwing whatever they could find at the stricken vehicle; and inevitably under such a vicious onslaught, the car soon ground to a halt.

But instead of everyone leaping towards the prone vehicle as I'd expected, nobody moved; in fact the Squirrels weren't even looking at the car. They were looking past it, at what seemed to be a cloud of boiling steam in the middle of the road. And as it billowed, I caught sight of what was causing it.

Breathing heavily through its nostrils and swinging its large black horned head rhythmically from side to side, its hooves pawing the ground, the Bull looked oblivious to everything around it, as if in a trance. Then suddenly the trance was broken and it was moving forward, the earth vibrating under its hooves with a dull, clumping sound, the noise becoming thunderous as the Bull gained speed; by the time it was maybe twenty feet from the car, only the screaming of the car's spinning wheels drowned it out. The Bull was perhaps ten feet away when somehow the car managed to break free of the junk on the road, lurch right onto the grass and out of the Bull's path, sending a dozen Squirrels up the nearest tree. Bumping along on the grass until it reached a point where the road was clear of obstructions, the car swerved back onto the tarmac and screamed off into the distance, dark grey smoke pouring from its exhaust.

Seconds after the car had fled, a muffled thud sounded somewhere back in the forest, followed by a groan. 'Sounds like Alvin didn't manage to stop in time,' a squeaky voice said from up a tree. 'We'd better go and see if he's okay.' The words were no sooner spoken than a posse of Squirrels with enough fur between them to make a hundred coats scurried off into the trees, while an equal number stood at the side of the road, chittering amongst themselves. A lone Squirrel, still armed with a fir cone and evidently bored with the chatter, walked out into the road. Looking in the general direction the car had gone, it bounced the fir cone off the ground in disgust before turning away.

And saw me, sitting there in the middle of the road.

It didn't keep the information to itself. Before I had a chance to blink it felt like I had half the Squizzes in the forest looking my way. With a gulp, I wondered if I was going to be some weird consolation prize because the Mastiff got away; and when the Bull appeared a few seconds later covered in twigs and leaves and surrounded by a gang of nut stealers, the thought only intensified.

As they made their way towards me I tried to look as nonchalant as possible. 'Hey,' I said, resting my arm on top of the car door, 'how's tricks?'

The Bull's voice was as deep as an underground cave. 'They've been better,' he said.

'Sorry to hear it,' I said, trying to keep things light. 'You hurt?'

'Hit a tree,' he told me. 'Well, I did after I hit the bramble. I've had worse.' Shaking his head, a pile of leaves and twigs rained down onto the Squirrels around him.

'Um... forgive me for asking,' I said, 'but what just happened?'

At first I thought he wasn't going to tell me. But after squinting at me for a while he said, 'The guy in the car – do you know him?'

'Not even his name. But I would like to talk to him.'

'I can help you with the first bit. His name's Hagen. We got past the talking stage a long time ago. Why do you want to talk to him?'

'This and that. Why do you want to kill him?'

'Tell him Alvin,' one of the Squirrels said excitedly. 'He might be a cop.'

'He ain't a cop,' the Bull said, shaking his head, his gaze not leaving mine.

'Maybe he's a Shamus,' another Squirrel said. 'You a Shamus, mister? You sure look like one.' Behind him, a few of the other Squizzes chuntered in agreement.

'Okay,' I sighed, with a well-practiced shrug. 'You got me.' Taking my license out of my pocket I flashed it around, getting several little 'oohs' as I did. I decided I liked the little guys.

Putting the license away I turned my attention back to Alvin.

'We weren't trying to kill him, just scare him enough to leave us alone,' the Bull said.

'Yeah – he thinks we're vermin,' a Squiz said, standing between Alvin's legs. 'They all do up there.' With the exception of the Bull, technically they were *all* vermin but I wasn't going to be the one to break it to them. Instead I nodded.

'There's probably been animals roaming around up there since the dawn of time, with no trouble,' another Squirrel, this one brandishing a pointed stick told me. 'Then *she* comes along and suddenly we're pests! Spoiling her land, she says. Her and Hagen and that other old son-of-a-bitch who does the dirty work for her.'

'Moseley?'

'That's him,' a smaller one piped up. 'When they first arrived he'd wait 'til it got dark and started taking pot-shots at us. Never hit any of us, though,' it finished, folding its paws across its chest.

This was starting to sound oddly familiar. 'Then what happened?' I asked.

'They used more extreme measures,' the Bull said. 'Started putting poison and traps down. Which is fine for us; we know to avoid them. But there's a lot of Olds roam about on that land. Or at least there were. We try to keep them away, but we can only do so much. And it isn't always enough.'

'They burn the bodies,' the Squiz between Alvin's legs said. 'And it ain't a pleasant smell. So we don't go up there much now.'

'Yeah. But to get to town they gotta get past us,' one at my feet holding a blowpipe chipped in. 'And we do what we can to remind them of that fact. That's the closest we've got to one of 'em yet,' he said proudly.

'You didn't say why *you* want to talk to Hagen,' the Bull said.

'Well, you're not the only ones being persecuted in this way.' I gave them a brief explanation. 'How many animals live up there?'

'Four that we know of. Her, Moseley, Hagen, and Dash, who looks after the grounds.'

'Scruffy Cat, not a lot to say for himself?'

'That's Dash.'

'We think he's deaf,' the Squirrel wielding the stick said.

'Deaf?'

'The only time we can get onto that land is when he's there on his own. As long as we don't walk right in front of him, he doesn't notice us.'

Recalling my own experience, I nodded. 'Before Hagen got here, did Moseley pass by?'

'If he had, he'd have got some of what Hagen just did.' So he had been in the basement after all.

'All this –' I indicated the mess on the road, 'must take a lot of planning.'

'Yeah,' the Bull said, something approaching a smile coming to his face. 'But it's worth it. Must cost them a fortune in car cleaning bills. And it's even more fun when it's Moseley chauffeuring her around – they both have short fuses.' His eyes glittered despite the gloom. 'But we have to be careful not to attack *every* vehicle that comes up here. I mean, if Bernie here had got his way earlier –' he looked down at the Squiz brandishing the stick '– you'd have got some of what Hagen just had.'

'When I passed by before – you were watching me?'

'We're always watching,' the Bull said, his voice even deeper than before.

While we'd been talking, a gang of Squirrels had been busy clearing the junk off the road. 'Thanks for your time,' I said to the Bull. 'And for not wrecking my car. I know you want to sort this thing out in your own way, but I'll leave one of these with you, just in case.' Opening my door I handed one of my cards to the nearest Squirrel, who after cooing over it for several seconds started passing it around, prompting even more cooing.

'I wish I was a Shamus,' one of them said wistfully. 'Plugging the bad guys, getting all the dames.'

'Aw, you read too many books,' another said. 'Whoever heard of a Squiz Shamus? It's probably not all it's cracked up to be anyway.'

'I never read a book in my life,' the wistful one squeaked. 'Where the hell would I keep a book dry out here?'

'Hey, I have books,' another said.

'Dry ones? Where'd you keep 'em?'

'Here and there. I'll let you borrow one if the price is right.'

'*If the price is right?* What a crock!'

'What's wrong with that? I got overheads to consider.'

As the babble of voices around me rose in pitch, it seemed like a good moment to go. Nodding to the Bull and waving to the Squizzes, I drove off.

Instead of going straight back to town I drove around for an hour or so, trying to think about everything that'd happened so far. When my belly started rumbling, I decided to give it up and get something to eat. Stopping in at the nearest roadside diner, I took a seat by the window and tucked into my food as thick black clouds gathered on the horizon. The next time I looked however the clouds had gone, replaced by an ever-darkening sky. Frowning, I looked at the clock on the wall of the diner and did a double take.

'Time flies,' I said to a waitress as she passed by.

'Sure does,' she said, smiling. 'Perhaps you should have a refill to keep you going.' She looked down at my coffee cup.

Then the penny dropped. 'I fell asleep?'

'Sure did,' she said, refilling my cup. 'Your nose was damn near in the gravy.'

Paying the bill, I went into the washroom and splashed cold water on my face. I was all in. I'd done more in the past day than I'd done in the past month. Not sure there was anything I could do now even if I'd been capable of doing it, I got in my car and drove home.

Despite my fatigue, on the way I managed to do a bit more thinking. Whatever I'd wandered into, my gut told me that it was something more interesting than a petty neighbourhood dispute; and not only that, it was going to take more than me to get to the bottom of it. So I decided: after a good night's sleep, I'd get up bright and early and give the Mouse a call, and get him doing something more interesting than a tail job for a change.

Something that for once might actually warrant a report.

7.

The Mouse – or to give him his real name, Linus Spayley – wasn't at home when I called; he was already at the office, waiting for me.

'Sounds like a lot of trouble to go to, to get rid of them,' he said when I'd finished telling him about the Chomsky's. 'What do you want me to do?'

'Head out to the woods and see if you can get any of those Squirrels to talk – they're a chatty bunch and they might know more than they think they do. Ask them if they've seen anyone else from the big house pass by. If they won't talk, show them your license and tell them you work for the Shamus they saw yesterday – after that, see if you can get them to shut up. Then go up to the Bouchard residence and try and get someone to come to the gate. If you can, chances are you won't get past them, and there's even less chance that they'll talk, especially if it's the gardener. The only way you'll get anything out of him is if you learn sign language first. But give it a go anyway.'

'Will do,' the Mouse replied as he left the office with a skip in his step. That's the kind of rodent he was.

He was still in reception when I heard a knock at the outer door, quickly followed by muted chatter between him and the new arrival before he left. A heartbeat later, when a large, Rabbit-shaped silhouette appeared on the glass of my door, I wondered which of the two bunnies had made the trip.

I took a guess. 'Come in, Harvey,' I called out.

I guessed right. Seeing the foot-long teeth, which he now kept in place by god knows what means, before I saw the creature they belonged to, I told him to take a seat, then looked away as he removed them.

It hadn't been much fun for him, back in the day when they'd been a permanent fixture in his mouth, not being able to eat, drink or talk properly; but it did mean that as an informer he was invaluable at picking up information other animals couldn't, because to most creatures Harvey was just a great big set of walking gnashers. Then, when he had them removed, it looked like I'd lost him; but realising he missed the excitement, he found a way of fastening the teeth back in his mouth. But as things turned out, informing wouldn't be the only excitement he got in his life.

'How did you know it would be me?' Harvey said.

I smiled. 'Lucky guess. So, what did you find out?'

'With regard to your clients, very little,' Harvey told me, gripping the outsized teeth in his fist. 'You probably know most of it. Known locally as Crying Willie and Flat-lugs Sascha –'

If I'd had a mouthful of coffee it would've ended up all over him. 'They're known locally as *what?*'

'Crying Willie and Flat-lugs Sascha. But I'm guessing not to their faces. The only thing of interest I found out was this business about the shooting of their brother.'

'And Mimi Bouchard?'

'Not much there either – at least on the surface. Runs a Salon, helps out at soup kitchens, that kind of thing – so clean she almost squeaks. But then I found out about what happened with Gwendoline Depledge.'

'Who the hell's Gwendoline Depledge?' I asked.

He was probably about half way through telling me when I buzzed for Taki to come in. Seeing the expression on my face, she looked uneasy. Looking across at Harvey, she glanced at the teeth in his fist and turned away.

She stood there impatiently as Harvey talked. When he'd finished I sighed, drummed my claws on the desk and looked her up and down for maybe ten seconds.

'*Well?*' she hissed eventually.

'Fine, thank you. I just wanted to see how beautiful you are.'

'Look,' she said, folding her arms, 'I've got work to do, so –'

'No, really – I wanted to see how beautiful you are. And you *are* beautiful. But that fur –' shaking my head, I tutted a few times.

'What's wrong with it?' she snapped.

'Well, it isn't you, is it? I need a secretary who's sassy, one who looks like she'd sock me on the jaw if I spoke out of turn.'

'Another crack like that,' she said, 'and I just might.'

'*I* know that and *you* know that, but what about everyone else? No, it's no good, sis – you need a new fur-do. And I know just the place you can get it. Who knows, this time they might even get it right.'

Giving her a run-down of how things stood, a slow smile came to her eyes. 'And this is all on expenses, right?'

'It is if the Chomsky's cough up.'

'I'll see if I can get an appointment,' she said, hurrying next door.

A few minutes later she came back. 'They've had a cancellation and can fit me in later this morning. One thing: what if I see the lady herself?'

'Tell her you decided to give them a second chance. Oh, and make sure the Chomsky's don't see you.'

'I'll get a cab to drop me right at the door. On expenses, of course.' Taking me off guard, she leaned across my desk and kissed me on the cheek. 'Bouchard's Salon, here I come.' Within a minute, she'd phoned for a cab, grabbed her things and left.

Settling up with Harvey, I asked him if he was going to put the money to good use. 'O yesh,' he said enthusiastically when the teeth were back in place.

Looking at his rumpled clothes and scuffed shoes, I couldn't help smiling. 'Well, don't blow it all at once. Bye, Harvey.'

'Vye,' he said, trying to smile back as he headed for the door.

Rather than going straight out, I decided to stay in the office a little while longer and enjoy the silence. Getting the cards out of the drawer, I laid them on the table and looked at the hand I'd been dealt. It was strange – I'd had nothing but silence for months and hadn't noticed it; now, for some reason it seemed important to drink it in and savour it, as if from now on silence would be in short supply.

After playing cards for a time, I realised that my heart wasn't in it. Leaving the hand unfinished, I grabbed my hat and coat, gave a big sigh, and left the office.

8.

Gwendoline Depledge... the name was almost as prepossessing as Mimi Bouchard. It conjured up images of grand theatrical dames, or ditzy young felines who flitted through life in a constant, excitable hurry.

Sometimes, it's cruel how wrong a name can be.

'She's a little short-sighted elderly Cat who used to live on Sebald Street,' Harvey had told me. 'First of all in a bus parked outside one of the houses, then after The Terror in the house itself. But it's the bus that seems to have caused all the trouble.'

'How?'

'In the Old days one of her owners was a bus driver, and when he retired the bus company let him keep his bus, so he brought it home and stuck it on the front lawn. Apparently it wasn't in the best condition then, but it's where the Old Gwendoline lived for over ten years. Anyhow, by the time The Terror occurred and Gwendoline moved indoors the bus was a rusting eyesore, but she couldn't bear to part with it. But it wasn't a problem because she was the only animal living in the street. Then one day Mimi Bouchard turned up.'

Pulling up in front of Higgins' Retirement Home, I noticed maybe a dozen furry faces watching me from various windows, some hopeful, some sad, the hopeful ones remaining hopeful right up to the moment they realised they didn't recognise me. Pretending I hadn't seen them, I went inside.

'You're in luck – Gwen's on good form today,' a member of staff informed me after letting Miss Depledge know she had a visitor. 'She says she'll see you. I'll take you through.'

Sitting in a high-backed chair against the wall of a large subdued room, an Airedale Terrier with thick grey fur peered in my general direction through pebbledash spectacles.

'Is this him?' she asked the assistant, sounding vaguely amused.

'This is him, Gwen,' the assistant replied. 'I'll leave you both to it.' Smiling, she did just that.

Indicating that I should take a seat, Gwendoline said, 'It's not every day I have nice young men asking after me, you know.'

Not having the heart to tell her she was wrong on all three counts, I said, 'My name's Spriteman. I'm a Private Investigator.'

'Well in that case young fella, I'd like to see your identification.' Proffering it, a pair of thin, grey paws appeared from under the green blanket on her knees. Grabbing hold of it, she held it up to her face. 'Not that I *can* see it that well of course,' she muttered as the card shook in her paws. 'Hang on. Ah yes: I've got it now. Well, Mr Spriteman – what can I do for you?'

After I'd explained why I was there, she looked down at her thin paws. 'Oh,' she said. 'That.'

She didn't speak for a while. But eventually she took a deep breath and began.

'I lived in that house and garden all my life,' she said, paws vanishing back under the blanket. 'Thought

I'd finish my days there too. Maybe if my eyes hadn't been so useless –' she shook her head.

I asked her to tell me what happened.

'What happened was that *she* knocked on my door one morning earlier this year to introduce herself as my new neighbour – not that she ever seemed to be there very often – I wasn't even sure which house she lived in. But she was friendly, you know – until she got the conversation onto the bus. Said how dreadful it must be, having that pile of garbage on my lawn and that she'd be *delighted* to get somebody to move it for me. When I told her I had no intention of letting *anyone* move it, she went away less than happy.

'After that she kept popping by – friendly on the surface like, you know, but always getting the talk back round to the bus. But I stuck to my guns, so the bus stayed where it was.

'Then one night, I heard noise outside, so I opened the curtains to look. I couldn't make 'em out that well, but there were a couple of Mutts near the bus. They must've seen me, because they went over to a truck parked further up the street and drove off sharpish. Next morning when I went outside, I found a rope attached to the back of the bus.'

'You didn't get much of a look at them though?'

'The Mutts? No. One of them was maybe bald, but I wouldn't swear to it.'

'What did you do?'

'Why, I called the police.'

'Anything come of that?'

'Na. Pair of dopes,' she mumbled. 'Didn't seem interested. Treated me like I was mad, said it was probably just someone's idea of a joke. Next day, the silent phone-calls started – heavy breathing, all that. I knew it had something to do with her. If it hadn't been for my damn eyes –' beneath the blanket, the paws knotted into fists.

'Been steadily getting worse for months – could barely see in front of me. Hadn't been able to leave the street for weeks. I had an appointment booked for the hospital a couple of days later, but with everything going on I'd forgotten all about it. Anyway, when the ambulance pulled up outside I had to go. I was only gone a couple of hours. But when the ambulance dropped me back here, the bus was gone.'

'In broad daylight?'

'Mine was the only occupied house in the street,' she said. 'Apart from *hers*. And when I asked her about it, she said she'd only just got back from town and hadn't seen a thing.

'Well – all the fight went out of me after that. Within a few days a letter arrived making me an offer on the house. Then not long after *she* came over, saying she wanted to "see how I was" –' Gwendoline widened her eyes at me, the effect rather startling through the thick lenses. 'And of course the conversation turned to the house…

'She was as nice as nice can be – saying that she'd take care of it all for me if I liked, and that rattling around in a big house like that on my own with dodgy peepers wasn't a great thing to be doing anyway. In a sense she was right; and as I say, the fight had gone out of me by then and I came round to the idea. So I let her get on with it. I got the money pretty quickly – in cash, I insisted on that – and got a cab to take me to the bank. Probably got less than it was worth, I realise that now, but it seemed okay at the time and I just wanted it to be over anyway.'

'What about paperwork?' I asked. 'Did you have to sign anything?'

'One or two signatures, but that was all.'

'Do you have proof of all this?'

She licked her teeth several times, then grimaced. 'I did, but in a fit of pique a few weeks ago I burned it all in the grate.'

'Do you remember what any of it said – names, anything like that?'

'No, not really. Company had a triple-barrelled name, though.'

'Could it be Wareham, Krukowski and Yang?'

'Could be. All these places sound the same to me. Anyway, I moved in here, and I like it. And maybe in some strange way it *was* the best thing to happen. But sometimes I think about *how* it happened and I can't get away from the fact that I was diddled – it was my *home*. Every once in a while I wonder if I shouldn't ask one of the staff to take me back there, just to have a quick look. But then I–' she waved the idea aside with her paw. A bit later she did the same thing with me, and fell into a long brooding silence. Thanking her for her time and getting no response, I left.

Consulting my worn-out map of the city, I realised that Gwendoline's old home wasn't as far away as I'd thought, but it still took me a while to find it – there was a uniformity about the streets which made me suspect that I was driving up and down the same one over and over. After a while I slammed on the brakes beside a middle-aged Labrador who was vigorously rubbing down a sedan with a chamois.

'I'm looking for Sebald Street,' I told him. 'But I think I'm going round in circles.'

'Yes, the houses round here do tend to look a bit samey, don't they?' the Labrador said, 'unless you look *really* closely of course.' He flashed me a smile so bright I didn't know how to respond to it. 'Carry on to the end of the road, and take the second right, then the first left. That's Sebald Street. Once visited, never forgotten.' Slapping the side of his car with the chamois, he smiled some more. With a slightly reluctant thank you, I drove away.

If Sebald Street had been empty when Gwendoline Depledge lived there, it certainly wasn't now; almost every house showed signs of occupancy. The gardens were well tended, the houses all freshly painted. I found what had been the Depledge residence maybe two-thirds of the way along, with freshly-laid slabs of turf out front, presumably where the bus had been. And like all the other houses, despite being nearly lunchtime, its curtains were closed.

Getting the new occupant out of bed and doing my best to ignore what she wasn't wearing, I asked a few questions and listened to what she didn't tell me, including the fact that she'd never heard of Mimi Bouchard. After that, I went to the house next door and went through the same routine; and, just to be on the safe side, a couple more houses after that, finding the same kind of householders and getting roughly the same responses from each. And not a single one of them claimed to have head of Ms Bouchard. And in the back of my mind, as the smile that Labrador had given me got wider and wider, I could only hope that Gwendoline Depledge didn't decide to come for a look after all, as I didn't think she'd like it very much if she did. Because although I couldn't be sure what Mimi Bouchard was planning for Montcrieff Terrace, on Sebald Street it was pretty obvious.

A jumped up madam Taki had called her.

She didn't know how right she was.

9.

Reminded as I was of my secretary, I headed over to Montcrieff Terrace with the hope of catching her coming out of the Salon, if she hadn't left already. Deciding that I wasn't ready to give the Chomsky's my news *just* yet, I parked up at the top end of the street and waited.

It was a relief not to find a taxi sat outside the Salon – fearing that my secretary might let this expenses business go to her head, I'd half expected her to tell the driver to hang around, no matter how long it took.

I only had to wait a couple of minutes when the door of the Salon opened and out stepped a feline who looked like she'd just spent a lot of someone else's money and enjoyed every second of it. Giving a quick rev on the engine, she spotted me. Walking briskly up the street, she put a paw up to her face as she passed the Pawnbroker's and hurried on.

'Beautiful,' I said, grinning as she climbed into the car.

'You like?' she grinned back, running a paw through her fur.

'I like. The way you made sure the Chomsky's wouldn't see you back there? I couldn't have done it better myself.'

'The fur,' she snapped. 'What do you think of the fur? It's cost you enough.'

'Well, it's cost Chomsky,' I corrected. 'Hopefully. Platinum blonde. Very nice. Uh-oh.' As I was speaking the door of the Pawnbroker's opened and Chomsky popped his head out. Turning the car quickly around in the road, I sped out of the street.

'You eaten?' Taki asked. 'I'll keep a look out for somewhere. Somewhere expensive, to go with the new look.'

'Don't push it,' I told her.

'You're all heart, Spriteman.'

'Tell me what happened at the Salon.'

'Well, I got a decent furdresser this time,' she said, patting her fur. 'And the atmosphere was better than last time, probably because *she* wasn't there. Not that the gal in charge today was any great shakes. I noticed her last time, hovering about – glasses, tight sweater – uptight, you know. Not the sort you'd want around at a party.' It sounded like Ms Vincent. 'And the rest of the staff kept their heads down.'

'What about the clientele – they tell you anything?'

'You mean the ones that hadn't nodded off under the dryers? There was only one. Phyllis she was called – and *she* barely stopped talking. Said she'd been going there since the place opened and liked it a lot – the girls were respectful, if a little timid, but she put that down to Ms Bouchard, who although very charming, did have a bit of a temper. Then she gave me an example: one time, this girl comes in, dolled-up to the nines and apparently drunk, asking for La Bouchard. Bouchard appears and ushers the girl into a back room where a screaming match starts, with most of the screaming being done by you-know-who. In fact the only thing Phyllis heard the girl say was that she worked for her. But Phyllis said she'd never seen the girl there before, and besides, she didn't look like she'd know one end of a pair of scissors from another.'

'Maybe she worked at another Salon,' I said.

'I said the same thing. But Phyllis seemed pretty sure that Mimi only has the one Salon. Strange, huh?'

'Did you ask about Gino?'

'Yeah, but she knew nothing about it and had never heard a Dog barking nearby. Having said that, I don't think her hearing was that great. Oh, and I tossed in a few remarks about the Salon being in such a shabby area, but she didn't reply. Anyway – that's it. Sorry it isn't more. So, what's going on there, do you think?'

'At the moment I doubt anything's going on. But that girl Phyllis heard having the argument with Mimi? I think she probably *does* work for her – just not in the Salon. And definitely *not* with a pair of scissors.' Deciding to brighten up my secretary's day even further, I elaborated a little.

'You're kidding?' she managed to say once she'd stopped laughing. 'Well, I've heard it all now. That's the absolute – hey, hang on; that looks *great*.' Pointing back at a 'deli we'd just passed, I managed to find a parking space close by. Then I noticed it was the kind of place that didn't have a pricelist in the window. Expenses-wise, today was turning into a heavy day.

The sandwiches were pretty good – or at least the bit I got to taste was. I was just about to take a second bite when the door of the 'deli burst open and a voice called out:

'Hey! Spriteman!'

Looking up, I saw Chomsky pushing his way through the tables. Dragging an empty seat over from the table next to ours, he sat down beside us. 'Didn't you see me waving at you back there outside the shop?'

'No,' I lied. 'Is it urgent?'

'Urgent? D'ya think I'd drive all over town looking for you if it wasn't? Boy, they look good,' he said, nodding at my plate.

'Help yourself.'

Picking up a sandwich in his nicotine-stained paws, he nibbled away at it for a time with his nicotine-stained teeth.

'So what's the big emergency?' I asked when the sandwich was almost gone. 'What's so important that you had to follow me across town?'

'To tell you this, I'd follow you halfway across the state,' he said, gulping back a mouthful of Taki's coffee. 'Wait 'til you hear it!'

'So tell me,' I said, losing my patience. 'What is it?'

'It's more like what it isn't,' he said, giggling a little. 'Your operative – Linus? Anyway, whatever he's called – he phoned up looking for you. He said to tell you that he *can't* go to the Bouchard place because it isn't there any more – it's been razed to the ground.' The Chihuahua's eyes sparkled with glee.

'Can I have another sandwich?' he said, reaching towards my plate.

10.

'So do you think he's been up here before?' Taki said, admiring herself in the passenger side mirror.

'Chomsky? Well, he seemed to know all about her house,' I said, checking my own mirror to make sure he wasn't following. 'But I don't think he's got anything to do with this. He's all hot air.' Still, it might be worth asking the inhabitants of the forest if they'd seen him skulking about.

In between polishing off our tuna sandwiches in the 'deli, he filled us in on what the Mouse had said.

'He got as far as he could, but there was a roadblock in place,' he told us, starting on my coffee once he'd finished Taki's. 'And he couldn't see much through all the smoke. Anyway, he headed to the nearest phone to let you know, but he didn't know where you were so he called me. Said he'd go back to see if he could find out anything else, and meet us up there.'

'"Us"?' I said. 'Oh no, you're not going.'

'What, you think I'd miss a thing like this?' Chomsky said, spitting crumbs everywhere. 'You bet your fat ass I'm going.' Taki stifled a giggle.

'You are getting a bit portly,' she said.

'Good thing I skipped lunch then,' I said, looking at my empty plate. 'Uh-huh. You're not going.'

I expected an argument but surprisingly didn't get one. 'Perhaps you're right, if there isn't that much to see,' he said, rising from the table. 'Besides, I gotta tell Sascha.' Whistling cheerfully, he left. Paying for the lunch I hadn't had I added a massive tip, knowing it was coming out of Chomsky's pocket.

We didn't even get into the heart of the forest when the car was enveloped by thick clouds of rolling smoke, the smell even penetrating the closed windows. Driving at a crawl, we strained our eyes looking for the Mouse's car. Eventually spotting it, I pulled in at the side of the road, and parked up in front of it. Perhaps hearing our approach, the Mouse appeared from among some trees further back and came towards us, looking flustered.

'I thought I'd try and talk to some of the critters in the woods, but the little devils keep running off,' he said, his face flushed. 'A lot of them have gone up to what's left of the house and are sitting in the trees, cheering and clapping. The fire crews have told them if they don't move back they'll turn their hoses on them.'

Thinking about what I'd seen them do yesterday, I remembered the talk about them being able to keep books dry, and wondered what else they could keep dry up there – matches, for example.

'How much further up can we go?' I asked.

'Not far before the police turn you back.'

'Is Dingus up there?'

'I didn't see him.'

'Might as well go up there anyway,' I said. 'You keep trying in the woods, see if you can catch up with any munchkins – they won't stay at the house forever.' The Mouse slunk back into the trees looking less than happy. I didn't blame him.

Before we got to the cordon a couple of cars passed us coming the other way, presumably Press and public disappointed that there wasn't more to see than the fire crews and a bunch of cops standing next to a line of tape coughing and spluttering. I looked hard but couldn't see Lieutenant Dingus among them.

'Coming for a look?' I asked Taki, pulling up well behind the tape.

'After what I've just paid to have my fur done? Forget it.'

Pressing a handkerchief over my mouth, I stepped out of the car.

With not as many trees up here as in the middle of the forest, the smoke didn't seem as thick, but it still stung my eyes. As it blew about I could see that the fire itself was pretty much extinguished apart from one area to the right where the majority of the fire crew were pointing their hoses. Uncomfortably, I realised it was this part of the house that I'd seen Mimi Bouchard in.

By the time I stepped back from the cordon, my throat felt like someone had shoved a toilet brush down it. Going back to my car a fire truck passed by, the resulting draft parting the smoke so I could see into the forest. Like the Mouse had said, the trees were chock full of Squizzes. But beneath them, watching the comings and goings with an expressionless face, was Alvin the Bull. With everyone's attention trained on what remained of the fire, I made my way over to him.

I got about a quarter of the way there when his eyes locked onto mine. 'It wasn't us, if that's what you're thinking,' he said.

'Perhaps,' I replied. 'But you all seem pretty happy about it.'

'Some of us are happy. Some are in shock. When the house blew up, all the windows exploded. Half the trees around here now have shards of glass imbedded in them. One chunk hit a tree a Squirrel was sleeping in and nearly took his head off. It's a miracle nobody's been hurt.'

'What time did the fire start?'

'No idea – none of us wear watches. First thing we knew about it was the explosion.'

'Was anyone up at the house?'

'Don't know and don't care,' he said, pawing at the ground.

'Thought you were always watching their comings and goings?' I asked.

'We decided to give it a rest for a while after yesterday. Plan our next move.'

I laughed at that. 'Something explosive next time, huh?'

'We didn't do it,' the Bull said, voice rumbling like thunder.

'Why should I believe you?'

'Because we'd have come up with something better than a fire,' he said before turning away.

'You believe him?' Taki asked when I told her what he'd said.

'I do. Although god knows what they'd have come up with that'd be worse than that fire.' I shuddered at the thought.

'So where now?' she asked.

'Back to the office.'

'My excitement's over for today, huh?'

''fraid so.'

'Ah well. It was good while it lasted.'

'Just how much *did* it cost?' I said, eyeing her up and down momentarily.

Smiling, she scribbled something onto a piece of paper I had lying around and held it up for me to see.

'*That* much?'

'*That* much,' she said, grinning.

'Well, let's hope the Chomsky's can stand for it,' I said, quickly turning my attention back to the road, 'or we'll have to get second jobs washing dishes.'

It was almost three o'clock by the time we got to the office, and while Taki made coffee I phoned police HQ.

'I might as well have gone up to the fire with you after all,' she said, sniffing at herself as I put the phone down. 'I stink. I don't think I'll ever get rid of this smell.'

'Hah. You should think yourself lucky,' I told her. 'If you think it was bad up there, you should smell where I'm going.'

11.

'Can I smell smoke?' Lieutenant Dingus said around his cigar as I entered his office.

'Yeah, it's coming from that thing sticking out of your mouth. I shouldn't worry about it.'

'No, this isn't cigar smoke.' As I sat down his nose started to twitch. 'This is different; it's fire smoke. Definitely. So unless I'm very much mistaken, I'd say you've been up at the Bouchard place.'

I was dumbstruck for a moment. 'How the hell can you smell *that* through all *this*?' I said, batting away cigar smoke.

'Oh, they're totally different,' he informed me earnestly. 'So, this fire – I'm guessing if you were there it wasn't an accident – if you see what I mean. Tell me about it.'

In truth, I wasn't really that surprised that he could tell the difference between different types of smoke or that he even knew about the Bouchard fire. Despite only holding the rank of Lieutenant and being so scruffy that most of the general public didn't believe he was a cop at all, Dingus was far and away the best the city had to offer. So when, as sometimes happens, a case went beyond my jurisdiction, I knew just the Basset Hound to turn to. And if passing on my knowledge helped my own little cases into the bargain, then that was all well and good too.

After explaining how I was mixed up in it all, I told him what I thought was going on. 'Basically, I think it's a property scam, but the end result looks to be extremely lucrative. Miss Bouchard, with the aid of her little band of heavies, finds out of the way streets with empty properties and moves in. Once she's done that she sets about taking control of these streets by leaning on anyone else living there using various threats and intimidation, and in the case of the Chomsky's, murder, with the aim of forcing them out. To aid this process, at some point an offer is made on the victims' property, which I'd imagine the victims are only too ready to accept. Then once she has these streets and houses to herself, she has *carte blanche* to do whatever she likes with them – in the case of Sebald Street, moving a different girl into every house who are then free to ply whatever trades they specialise in – and if the girls I spoke to are any indicator, I'm guessing that none of them specialise in standing around cutting fur.' Here the Lieutenant widened his eyes. 'And with the Chomsky's out of the way she'd be free to do the same thing on Montcrieff Terrace. Unluckily for her, instead of rolling over they decided to do something about it.'

Not long after I started speaking the Lieutenant began nodding his head, causing his large ears to flap. At certain points while I was talking they were damn near causing a draft.

'You know what I think?' he said, cigar smoke billowing away from him, 'this has Ballbag Betty stamped all over it.'

When I spluttered my reply it wasn't because of cigar smoke. '*Who*?'

'The name threw me at first, but it sounds like that's who it is. Around six months after The Terror she was arrested when she was involved in a barroom brawl with two other girls over a small-time hood name Marvin Falconetti, who was rumoured to be running girls in the area. It took three officers to bring her in, she was spitting and screaming so much. Her party trick was putting pool balls in socks and whacking anyone she didn't care for around the head with them. One of the two ladies she got in a fight with went home missing half her teeth, while the other was in the hospital for a fortnight. The feline with the sock, a Chartreaux with a heart-shaped face, gave her name as Betty. Later, when a rumour went round the station the balls found in the sock didn't come off a pool table, it was only half dismissed. A tough cookie to be sure.'

'Sounds like she's come up in the world since then,' I said. 'But if it is Mimi, then she must have a criminal record.'

Dingus pulled a face like he was suffering from trapped wind. 'Under normal circumstances yes,' he said. 'But we didn't have her that long. This Falconetti, her "boyfriend" as she called him, came and got her out not long after she was brought in; probably slipped someone something to forget the whole thing – you remember what the force was like back then. But because of the incident with the sock, nobody did forget. But after that we never saw either of them again. The assumption was Falconetti had left town and she'd gone with him.'

'Only now she appears to be back, perhaps without Falconetti.' *If she wasn't in the fire,* I thought.

'Hmm,' Dingus said, nodding once more. Eventually he stopped and picked up his phone. 'Warren? Dingus. How many officers can you spare tonight?' After relating the tale I'd just told him, he listened for a while. 'That's all? Well, send them up to Sebald Street, but keep two back; they can come with me to Montcrieff Terrace. Yes, that's fine. Bye.' He put the phone down. 'All set for eleven o'clock,' he said, clapping his paws together. 'I take it you'll be coming along? Good, good. That's good...' suddenly the Lieutenant couldn't look me in the face. 'Look Benji, don't take this the wrong way,' he began, turning his attention to the new cigar he was unwrapping, 'but you might want to take a bath before we go there tonight. I hate to say it, but you're a bit on the ripe side.'

For several seconds I tried to respond but the words wouldn't come. Speechless, I shook my head and rose, leaving the Lieutenant and his vile stogies behind.

12.

Taking the Lieutenant's less than subtle advice, I went home and climbed into the tub for a long soak, but no matter how hard I scrubbed the smell wouldn't go away. Putting on a clean set of clothes, I did my best to ignore it. Next, I tried to get rid of the taste of smoke, along with the hunger pains, by proceeding to empty half my fridge and four cups of coffee into my stomach. The hunger pains vanished; the taste of smoke remained. Suitably fed and watered, I headed back across town.

Pulling up in Montcrieff Terrace behind the Lieutenant's car just before eleven, it was eerily quiet and dark. Of all the streets' lamps only one worked properly, the one outside the bar. A second just ahead of the Chomsky's place fizzed on and off every few seconds.

Seeing me approach Dingus got out of his car, followed by two officers. Thanks to the flickering light, we were able to time our movements so we could get past the Chomsky's without being seen. In the room above the store, a yellow light burned behind a curtain. Ahead, the Salon was in darkness.

'Ready?' Dingus asked. I nodded. Then he turned

to the two officers. 'Okay – Freeman, you keep an eye on the street but stay out of sight. Mulcahy – be ready here at the front door. I shout, you come running. Got that?' Mulcahy nodded. 'Okay. Now…'

As the Lieutenant turned away, I was in the process of asking him how we were going to get inside when there was a sharp click and the Salon door popped open.

'Now can you believe that?' Dingus said, slipping something metallic back into the pocket of his trench coat. 'Some animals just don't give a damn about security. I can't understand that. Oh well. Shall we go in?' Clicking on a flashlight, he stepped inside. Switching on my own, I followed.

This time round the place didn't seem to smell so bad, perhaps because I stank of smoke. But for the Lieutenant, whose sense of smell was perhaps his best asset, it was all a bit much.

'You're right,' he said, spluttering through the dirty handkerchief he had clamped to his nose and mouth as he looked at the framed newspaper clippings on the walls, 'she certainly knows a lot of well-connected individuals.'

While he gawped and coughed, I went over to the curtain I'd seen Miss Vincent go through the last time I was here. When I popped my head around it and nobody stuck a gun in my ear, I figured it was safe to proceed. A couple of seconds later, Dingus joined me.

Shining our lights around in the small corridor, we found three doors. Behind one was nothing but a closet full of cleaning utensils. The sturdy door to the right we figured led out to the rear of the property. Deciding to leave it until last we tried the third door, hoping it led upstairs.

When it did, it's safe to say that what we found up there took me by surprise. Flicking a few switches, the large open-plan space was bathed in a dim red light, revealing a room full of deep leather seats and the sweet aroma of stale perfume. Dotted around on a few tables were empty champagne flutes, a couple smeared with lipstick.

Neither of us said a word. At the rear of the room another door opened onto more stairs, at the top of which were a couple of small bedrooms, while most of the other rooms were clearly in the process of being turned *into* bedrooms, presumably for more girls to work from once the Chomsky's had been forced out.

'Well,' Dingus said, 'not much business going on yet maybe, but it looks like a Cathouse, all right.'

'So she's already started,' I said. 'She didn't even wait until the Chomsky's were gone. But how the hell haven't they noticed? They must have spotted something, surely.'

'They didn't spot us coming down the street,' Dingus said. 'They can't spot everything. But I agree, it is unusual.'

Heading back down the stairs, we opened the door we'd left earlier, which did indeed lead out to the rear of the property. In the past it must've served as the buildings' parking area, accessed via the sides of the building, but these spaces were now blocked off by several large plant pots on either side, leaving a large, empty quadrangle. At its rear, a large hedge blocked the view to whatever lay beyond.

'What's on the other side of the hedge?' I wondered.

'Beats me,' Dingus said. 'We'll take a look on the way out.' Suddenly he froze. 'You hear that?'

Listening closely, I did: the low rumbling of a car's engine close by. I'd just realised where it was coming from – the other side of the hedge – when the hedge itself was flooded with bright white light. Then, under the sound of the engine we heard what sounded like a car door opening, quickly followed by a sharp, metallic click. Before either of us could wonder what was going on, we watched as the entire hedge started to move in one fluid motion inwards, towards us.

Looking quickly for somewhere to hide, we dashed around to the side of the building and the large plant pots just as the hedge swept past us, resting against the wall to our left. From where we hid we could see that it wasn't a hedge at all, but a very long gate covered on one side with foliage. A few seconds later, the nose of an expensive-looking car edged into the quadrangle.

Once he'd parked, the driver – a dandified, middle-aged Deerhound with long, grey fur and a blood-red flower in the buttonhole of his grey suit – turned off his lights and engine and got out of the car, carrying a bunch of flowers. Glancing around, he seemed puzzled. With a shrug, he locked his car and moved towards the back door.

We got there before him. 'Hey, who are you?' he asked. 'Where is everyone?'

'You know, that's just what I want to know sir,' Dingus said, taking him by the arm. 'Perhaps you can assist me on that matter. Mulcahy!'

Mulcahy dashed around the side of the building. 'Yes sir?'

'Take Mr –'

'Shoebury,' the Deerhound said, unruffled. 'Lance Shoebury.'

'– Take Mr Shoebury here inside. And send Freeman round here.'

As Shoebury was led away, Dingus went back over to look at the gate/hedge.

'Crafty,' he said, eventually finding the gate's catch

amongst the foliage. 'I wonder where it leads to...' he began rubbing one of his ears distractedly.

He was still doing it when Freeman appeared. 'Yes, Lieutenant?'

'Remove those pots from the side of the building and bring my car round here,' he said.

While he waited, Dingus walked through the open gate, disappearing from view. I was just about to join him when I heard his car approaching.

When he reappeared he had a curious expression on his face. 'Okay Benji,' he said, clapping his paws together, 'let's go on a little trip.' Getting into his car, the first thing the Lieutenant did was switch his lights to full beam. Then, very slowly, he turned right and inched us forward.

For the next twenty minutes or so, we never really got beyond inching. The road – or rather the long stretch of concrete that had once been a road – was covered in every kind of trash imaginable, from broken furniture and sacks of garbage to unwanted building materials and abandoned cars. But with careful navigation Dingus was able to follow what was a narrow route of sorts through the debris.

'What on earth *is* all this?' I said as we drove past a particularly perilous-looking heap of garbage that looked like it might topple on top of us.

'An abandoned freeway,' Dingus said. 'Probably been like this since The Terror. Remember at first how nobody knew where to put their trash before the refuse services started up again? It got dumped *everywhere*. And I guess if this road wasn't used much anyway, it was the perfect place. I've heard of whole *areas* still like this, not just roads, even now.'

Eventually among all the crap Dingus's lights flashed across a section of rusted metal fencing, through which was what appeared to be another section of road. Parking up beside it, it was apparent that the fence had been put there with the express purpose of blocking off the debris-strewn section of the freeway from its neighbour. Moving it out of the way, we stepped out onto a garbage-free section of road, where within a few seconds, a couple of cars drove past us into the night.

'Looks like she's created her own private road for those in the know,' Dingus muttered. 'Enterprising.'

'Certainly explains why the Chomsky's haven't noticed anything,' I said.

'Hmm. Okay. Let's head back.'

Turning the car in the narrow spot between the garbage and garbage-free roads, we juddered our way back through the junk towards the Salon. As we approached and Dingus's lights lit up the back wall, I saw that some parts of the brickwork were less faded than others, the result of removing a metal staircase from the wall. For the briefest of moments, something inside me flipped over and a chill passed through me.

'I wonder how things are going at the raid,' Dingus said, driving along the side of the Salon and back onto the street. 'Hello?' He shouted into his radio, but there was no response. 'Hello?' Shaking his head, he whacked it against the dashboard, and it crackled into life. 'Hello!' he bellowed again. '… Blevins? Is that you?'

'*Yes, it's me Lieutenant,*' a distant voice replied. '*Can you hear me? It's not a great line.*'

'Yeah, I can hear you. How's it going?'

'*Jackpot, Lieutenant. Nearly two dozen arrests, girls and customers alike.*'

'You had any trouble?' the Lieutenant shouted amid the blare of white noise.

'*Only one minor incident, sir,*' Blevins said, his voice threatening to cut out at any second. '*We attracted a bit of a crowd, and – hello? Can you –? ...anyway, one of the locals recognised her other half being led away in cuffs. She wasn't very happy about it, so she hit Officer Yallop with her purse. But then she realised where her other half had been and... hit with her purse too... hello, Lieutenant? You still there?'*

'Just about,' Dingus said as the radio whined feedback. 'Get them all back to the station, and – hello? *Hello!'* at that point, the radio gave up completely. 'It's okay most of the time,' he said, putting it down. 'I keep asking for a new one but I never get it. Freeman!'

Freeman appeared. 'Sir?'

'Patrol the area until the end of your shift then get someone else to take over. If anyone interesting turns up, I want to hear about it. Meanwhile, I think it's time we got Mr Shoebury bedded down for the night.'

'You going to question him first?' I asked.

'No, he can wait 'til morning. All that perfume earlier's given me a headache. See you later, Benji.'

As he, Mulcahy and Lance Shoebury puttered off up the street in Dingus's car, the front door of the Pawnbroker's opened. With everything else going on I hadn't even thought about the Chomsky's. But instead of Crying Willie coming out to see what all the fuss was about it was Sascha standing there, rubbing her paws together and looking even more agitated than usual.

'Oh, Mr Spriteman, thank goodness you're here,' she said. 'Have you seen Willard? He hasn't been home since he left this afternoon. I thought he might have stopped in at Kowalski's but the car's not here, and –'

'Have you been in to check?'

'No,' she said. 'I – I don't like to go in there on my own. But if the car isn't here –'

'I'll go over there anyway,' I said, trying to calm her down. 'Maybe he parked the car round the corner.' I wasn't hopeful, but the idea that the little yap was in a bar somewhere, celebrating Miss Bouchard's misfortunes sounded more than plausible.

Luckily, the first thing I heard when I entered Kowalski's was Chomsky, holding court at the bar. The barkeep looked thoroughly sick of him.

'Hey – Spriteman!' he shouted when his eyes uncrossed long enough to spot me. 'C'mere, c'mere. I've been telling everyone how Miss Boo-shard finally got what was coming to her. Hey, how about a drink? On me. You wanna drink?'

'Wrong species,' I reminded him. 'Besides, your nearest and dearest is wondering where the blazes you are.'

'My nearest and –? Ah, you mean Shasha! You know, I haven't even told her yet.' He shook his head and looked regretful, in that way only drunks can. 'I *should've* told her, but I haven't.'

'Well, let's put that right shall we?' I said, grabbing him under the arms and propelling him towards the door.

Because I'd taken him by surprise, he didn't start to get belligerent until we were outside. 'Hey, what'sa hurry?' he mumbled, struggling in my grip. 'Getcha filthy paws offa me.'

'Not until you're safely home,' I told him. 'Come on, Thumbelina.'

He was only half-conscious by the time I got him to the Pawnbroker's, and despite his size he was becoming a dead weight. Luckily, Sascha opened the door before I lost my grip on him.

'What on earth – oh, Willard!' she said as he stumbled inside, belching. 'Look at the state of you!'

After helping her get Chomsky up to bed, I stood outside on the street and wondered what to do next. Although it was late I didn't feel like going home, didn't feel in the least bit tired. So instead of hitting the hay I drove round the city, like I'd been doing for the past few months. And as I did I realised something: unlike my previous nightly excursions, this time I was enjoying myself; or more precisely, enjoying being back on a case. Slowly, it felt like I was coming back to life.

It wasn't until I eventually did call it a night that my mood began to change, and I started to think about Dingus's car lights earlier, shining onto the Salon's back wall – a wall which at some point had had a metal staircase bolted to it, which in turn reminded me of *another* metal staircase, one with a Toucan standing in front of it, its sharp beak lunging towards the ground, the image jagging away at me like pins in a new shirt. What *was* it that it reminded me of?

Wearing myself out with it, I fell into an uneasy sleep.

13.

'The Fire Chief just called the station. The overnight rain has helped to put out the fire at the Bouchard residence. But before it did *another* fire started up in the basement and they've uncovered something. Shall I meet you over there?'

Normally the thought of wading knee-deep through wet ash wouldn't have appealed, but there was something in Dingus's voice which changed my mind. 'I'll be there as soon as I've had a wash and brush up,' I told him.

'Good. Oh – and you might want to bring something to put over your nose.' He hung up.

I was still some distance from the Bouchard place when I found out what he meant; it was still smoke, but this time around the aroma was different; rich and sweet, an aroma I usually associated with illegal drinking dens and the backrooms of jazz clubs. Winding up my window, I remembered the girl in the Salon Phyllis had seen, and wondered maybe if she hadn't been drunk after all.

Passing the spot where I'd seen the Mouse's car the day before, I was surprised to see it there again. Pulling in behind it, I braced myself by taking a breath of relatively clean air before stepping out of the car.

Looking around I saw nothing but heard plenty, mostly a rapid chittering hidden among the greenery. Then I heard rough footsteps, making their way towards me. When the Mouse appeared, he didn't look his best – his fur was dripping with sweat and his face was covered in black streaks, his eyes glowing in the forest's semi-darkness.

'Linus, what are you doing here –'

'Well, I couldn't find anyone who'd talk to me yesterday, so I thought I'd come this morning and try again,' he said. 'But today it's even worse! Whenever I get close enough to a Squirrel to ask anything, they run up the nearest tree and start giggling! They seem to think the whole thing is one big joke. One of them even threw mud at me! What's *wrong* with them all?' he squeaked, rubbing his dirty face and making it even dirtier. 'And what's that *smell*?'

At that moment I couldn't think how to explain it to him. Instead I said, 'Look, forget about them for a while. Apparently they've found something up at the house – let's go and take a look.' Staggering back to his car he led the way, his driving rather erratic. Luckily for him, nothing was coming the other way.

As we arrived, the Lieutenant spotted us and came over.

'Quite a stink, huh?' he said, wafting the smoke around with his paw. 'They thought they had the whole thing under control but then the fire got into the basement and put paid to what must've been a pretty big exotic plant collection. Too much for personal use, wouldn't you say?'

'Certainly. But you didn't get me up here for that, I hope?'

He shook his head. 'Uh-huh. I got you up here because of the bodies – two of them.'

Glancing over at the Mouse, I decided he was in no fit state to look at corpses. Telling him – if at all possible – to get some fresh air in his lungs, I followed Dingus through the cordon over to where the house had stood.

'The Fire Chief thinks kerosene was poured around the perimeter of the building then ignited,' Dingus said. 'The whole place would've been alight in seconds.'

'Where were the bodies found?'

'One in the basement, the other near the perimeter. Maybe whoever it was started the fire didn't get away quick enough. The remains have been taken down town. But the one in the basement's interesting because it's in such good condition. Chances are it's been down there a while, too.'

Getting helmets and masks from the Fire Chief, we tramped through the saturated but still oddly brittle foundations of the house over to a large, black rectangular maw in the ground surrounded by rubble, a flight of ash-coated concrete steps leading down into thick darkness.

'Be warned,' the Fire Chief told me. 'It isn't pretty.' Flicking on his flashlight, we followed suit and headed down the steps.

It didn't feel so much like walking into a waterlogged cellar as a trench at the bottom of the ocean. Initially, there was nothing to see except the flecks of ash swirling in the beams of our flashlights, but further in details began to present themselves; fragments of debris, walls that looked like they were caked in crusted silt, the damp carpet of ash covering the floor. In what felt like slow motion we padded over to the far side of the basement.

'Okay,' the Fire Chief said, 'here it is.'

Playing the beam of his flashlight across the floor, a grotesque and twisted greyish-green lump appeared in the gloom. After a couple of seconds I was able to make out features: a patch of fur, an ear, a heart-shaped face –

I was looking into the face of Mimi Bouchard.

'But –' I started, 'how –'

'Because it isn't her, Benji,' Dingus said. 'This one's been down here some time, remember. And the reason it's probably so well preserved is because it was hidden away in that.'

Pointing his flashlight beam over to the right, it lit up a small pile of junk nearby. 'What's left of a barrel,' he said. 'The fire crew came down when they thought the fire was out and spotted it burning away in the corner. When they turned their hoses on it, it split open and the body fell out. Gives me a chill just thinking about it.'

'But it looks just like her,' I said, still dazed. 'So if it isn't Mimi, who the hell is it?'

'Well, unless I'm mistaken, I'd say we're looking at what's left of Marvin Falconetti.'

'I don't understand.'

'Neither did I at first. When I heard that a body had been found and asked for a description I assumed it must be Mimi too. But after hearing how long it had been down here, I knew it couldn't be her. So who was it? Then I started to think about Falconetti – whatever happened to him? Where is he now? I didn't see him that night he was at the station but I asked an officer who did what he looked like. Not only could he tell me, but it turned out Falconetti had been in before on a previous occasion and had a mugshot taken.' Rooting around in one of his larger pockets, he pulled out a photograph. 'And it's fair to say it gave me a start.'

Taking it from him, I shone my light onto it and found myself staring at a cool but dangerous-looking black Chartreaux with slicked-back fur, luminescent eyes and a heart-shaped face.

'Creepy, huh?' Dingus remarked.

'It must've been like looking in a mirror,' I muttered.

'From what you've told me, maybe that was part of the appeal.'

'Until she bumped him off and stuck him in a barrel.' Looking over to the charred wood close to the body, a chill went up my spine. 'So if there's only two bodies and this is Falconetti... who's the other one? I don't believe for one second it's Mimi.'

Dingus turned to me sharply. 'You don't? Why?'

'Because she's too smart,' I said. 'I think maybe I was getting too close for comfort, and she decided to cut her losses and split. I think she set the fire. Or rather, one of her associates did.'

'Then we'd just assume it was her,' Dingus finished. 'I suppose it's possible. But say it *wasn't* her – that leaves two possibilities – the Chomsky's, or the munchkins in the forest.'

I shook my head. 'I don't think it was anybody in the woods, the amount of damage that was caused. They'd have taken that into account. You don't mess on your own doorstep. As for the Chomsky's – well, maybe he'd *talk* about stuff like that, sure, but actually do it? I don't think so. Look, can we get out of here? This place is starting to give me the creeps.'

Silently, we trudged back up to *terra firma*. Removing our masks, the smell was as strong as ever. 'It's the Squirrels I feel sorry for,' the Fire Chief said, looking over towards the trees. 'They've been inhaling this stuff a lot longer than we have. Those little fellas are going to have pretty sore heads later on.'

'Right; time I headed back to the station,' Dingus said. 'A lot of animals from last night to deal with.'

'I don't envy you. Me, I've got a Dog killer to catch.' Saying our goodbyes, we made our way to our cars.

I found the Mouse standing next to his. He still looked green around the gills.

'I'm going to the office,' I said. 'Why don't you come back and take it easy for a while? You look all in.'

'I *am* all in,' he said.

'Okay to drive?' He nodded. Taking no chances, I decided to drive in front this time; that way, I could keep a better eye on him.

Getting to the office without incident, Taki took one look at us and went to put on some coffee.

'Milk for me,' the Mouse said, slumping in a chair.

'Give him it warm,' I said to her quietly. 'So – anything come in yet?'

She opened her mouth to reply when the phone rang. 'First call of the day,' she said. Sitting on the edge of her desk, I grabbed the phone. 'Hello, Spriteman Detect –'

'Mr Spriteman?' A trembling voice said. 'It's – I – I don't know what to do, I –'

It took me a second or two to realise who it was. 'Sascha, calm down. What's wrong?'

She tried to tell me, but she spoke so quickly the only word I caught clearly was 'outside', which she repeated several times. 'Sascha, listen to me. I'll come over right away. Just try and keep calm.' I put the phone down.

The Mouse was standing in front of me now. 'What's wrong?' he asked.

'I don't know. But she's in a terrible state. Hopefully it'll be nothing worse than her brother's hangover.'

'But you're not sure,' he said. 'Want me to come along?'

I thought about it. 'Yes. But I'll drive.'

Because of the urgency in Sascha's voice I found myself driving quicker than I normally would.

'It's funny, being in the same car again,' the Mouse said as I moved up through the gears. 'Like the old days.'

'Only with me driving you around. Did you just say *old* days? That was less than a year ago.' Looking over at him, his eyelids had started to droop. Minutes later he was fast asleep and snoring, a surprisingly formidable sound for someone who a few years earlier could've fitted inside a matchbox.

'I don't know,' I tutted to myself. 'The Mice of today.' He didn't wake up until we got to the Pawnbroker's, sluggish and bleary-eyed.

We weren't even out of the car before Sascha came rushing towards us. She looked distraught.

'He – he's round the back,' she managed to say, her voice breaking. 'In the alley. He's –' putting a paw up to her mouth, she stifled a cry.

Following her round the side of the building, the body was lying face up in the garbage, its clothes dishevelled and covered in blood. Behind us, Sascha started making an odd wailing noise.

'Take her inside,' I said to the Mouse.

'Come on Miss Chomsky,' he said softly, ushering her gently towards the back door.

They were still a couple of feet away when the door burst open and a figure emerged, not looking much better than the corpse. 'What's going on?' Chomsky said, resplendent in a pair of yellowing long johns. 'And what the hell's all the racket about out here?'

14.

Leaving Chomsky to take Sascha back inside, the Mouse and I followed them in. 'Would – would anyone like coffee?' she asked. No-one answered. 'I'll go and make some anyway,' she muttered. Nodding to the Mouse, he trotted after her into the kitchen.

Groaning, Chomsky slumped down into a battered old armchair, clutching his head in his paws.

'Bad hangover, huh?'

'The worst,' he said, rubbing his face. 'Um, I'm going to get dressed. I'll be back down in a minute.' He slunk out of the room.

Alone, I reflected on how the atmosphere in the house didn't sit right, even taking the corpse behind the property into account. And unless my mind was playing tricks with me, I was pretty sure the last time I saw Chomsky he hadn't had a gash above his right eye. And then there was the identity of the victim...

Despite not liking the way my thoughts were running, I called the cop shop and asked to be put through to Dingus, hoping that he'd be too busy to talk to me. But a couple of seconds later his cracked-leather voice was in my ear.

'Dingus.'

'I don't want to drag you away from something important, but you might want to get down to Montcrieff Terrace ASAP.'

'Serious?'

'Serious enough for you to bring Clancy along,' I told him. 'Mitch Moseley's body's lying out here in the alleyway. I thought you were having a cop patrol the area last night?'

There was a long pause. 'I'll be right over,' he said.

Putting the phone down I turned to see Chomsky, now fully dressed. Was it my imagination, or did he look scared? I decided it wasn't my imagination.

'Heavy stuff all this,' he said in a forced voice. I nodded.

'Where did you end up after you left us yesterday?' I asked. 'Your car isn't out on the street.'

'I decided to stop in at a bar on the way home. I only intended to have one, but...' he shook his head. 'Anyway, when I got out of there I was in no fit state to drive, so I got a cab. When it pulled into the Terrace I saw a couple of guys I knew going into Kowalski's so I decided to, you know, have one for the road.'

'Only you didn't stop at one.'

'You want a hangover this bad, you have to put in the effort.' He tried to smile.

'That looks nasty,' I said.

'Huh?'

'That cut above your eye. It wasn't there when I brought you home.'

Raising a paw to the cut he touched it, winced.

'Maybe I fell or something. During the night.'

At that moment Sascha and the Mouse came back in, and Chomsky left the room once more. 'Coffee, Mr Spriteman?' she asked.

'Thank you. I don't suppose you heard anything last night?'

She blinked a few times and looked even more timid than usual. 'No, nothing. After you helped me put Willard to bed I went to bed myself. I was worn out with it all by then.' Finishing her coffee in silence, she went back into the kitchen.

I looked over at the Mouse. 'Anything?'

He shook his head. 'Not a word,' he said.

Chomsky still hadn't come back in when Dingus turned up, followed by the city's meat wagon. Reluctantly, I filled him in on the details, during which time he said nothing. I didn't know if that was a good sign or not.

'So what happened to the patrol?' I asked.

'Understaffing is what happened. Apparently Freeman couldn't get anyone to take over at the end of his shift, so he stayed on for a while. Then word came through of a robbery in progress a few miles away and there was no-one else who could take it so he had to –'

'Who's this?' I interrupted.

'Oh,' Dingus said, following my gaze. 'That's the Coroner.'

He was a small, stocky middle-aged Tabby in an off-white jacket, with thick fur and thick glasses to match. Nodding his greeting he walked past us, whistling tunelessly to himself. Standing over the body, he sighed.

If anything, Moseley's mean little face looked even meaner in death, his jutting chin pointing up at us defiantly. Despite the fight he must've been in, his cap remained in place. When the coroner removed it, a crinkled little bald head was revealed.

Crouching beside the corpse and blocking our view, the Coroner stopped whistling. 'Nasty,' he muttered. 'Throat's been cut.' Moving round on his heels slightly, he opened Moseley's shirt and began prodding at his midriff, the way you'd prod at a loaf of bread to test if it was fresh. 'Looks like he's been punched, too.' Then he stood up. 'Okay fellas,' he said, looking at the animals who'd followed him round, 'away you go...' Moving aside, we watched as the Coroner's assistants worked in silence, first taking pictures before loading the body onto a stretcher and placing it in the back of the meat wagon. As all this was going on, the Coroner sat up front in the passenger seat, staring straight ahead. Seconds later, the remaining animals piled in, and, without a word, drove out of the alley and up the street.

'What happened to Clancy?' I asked.

'Unavoidably delayed. That boat of his that he's so proud of? Well, last night it sank – with him in it. Luckily it was still in the marina. He's okay but I imagine the mood he's in it's probably best he wasn't here for this one. But with Teo on leave, Ashton's ordered him to come in as soon as he can. Did you notice a smell back there?'

'Nothing out of the ordinary. So who was –'

'Plummer.'

'I've never heard of him,' I said.

'Until today neither had I. He was drafted in at the last minute. Um, Benji – you know what's going to happen here.'

'You're going to take Chomsky in for questioning.'

'What choice do I have? Someone kills his brother and he says he knows who did it. Not long after, that someone turns up dead outside his house. And not only that, it sounds like he's been in a fight.'

As Dingus spoke I realised why I'd told him all this in the first place – because despite how it all looked, I didn't believe that Chomsky had done it. 'Oh, come on, Dingus. You heard what the coroner said about the body. A little guy like Chomsky couldn't do that.'

'He could with a belly full of beer inside him.'

'But –'

'Save your breath, Spriteman,' Chomsky said, joining us in the alley.

A moment later Sascha appeared, looking confused. 'Willard,' she said. 'What's going on?'

'I'm just going to the police station to answer a few questions is all,' Chomsky told her, patting one of her paws. 'The sooner we get this cleared up, the better things will be. Okay – ready when you are, Lieutenant.'

Heading round to the front, me, Sascha and the Mouse watched in silence as the two small Dogs got into the Lieutenant's car and drove off.

'I should go keep an eye on the shop,' Sascha said distractedly, worrying her paws. 'Keep busy; you know. The sooner this is cleared up the better, like Willard says. If – if you'll excuse me –' Raising a paw to her mouth, she hurried back inside, slamming the door behind her.

'It doesn't look good for him, does it Mr S?' the Mouse said.

'No. Do you think he did it?'

He thought about it for a second. 'Nah. I don't think he's got it in him.'

'My sentiments exactly. Look, go back and get your car, go home and get cleaned up. Then check Chomsky's movements from leaving us yesterday until he treated us to a view of his underwear this morning. Also, have a word with Sadie, see if she heard anything last night. Oh, and contact Harvey – see what he knows about Falconetti – or anything else for that matter.'

'Where will you be?' the Mouse asked.

'I have absolutely no idea,' I said.

As he drove off I decided to go to the station, realising that I'd forgotten to ask Dingus if he had any new information which could help me.

'No, nothing,' he said, looking surprised to see me again so soon. 'Although we have managed to track down the manageress of the Salon, Miss Vincent. She should be in shortly. Actually, while you're here...' rubbing at one of his large, leathery ears, he looked at me hopefully, 'You could do me a favour. That guy we pulled in last night, Shoebury? Well, I haven't had a chance to talk to him yet. Now I could hand him over to another officer, but like I said we're short staffed at the moment, and I really need to talk to Chomsky now and you *were* there, so... what do you say?'

Pretending that I had something better to do I eventually said, 'On one condition – I get to speak to Vincent when she gets here.'

Dingus wasn't fooled for a second. 'Oh, I think we can manage that,' he said, a wry smile playing across his face.

15.

The station's bullpen was heaving with animals from the raid, the girls looking defiant, the males scared. They stood in corners, sat on chairs, on unoccupied desks. The cramped conditions had turned the place into a hothouse – the air stank of stale sweat and perfume, cigarettes and reeking animal fur; the drone of bored chatter was occasionally enlivened by the odd pistol crack from a wad of burst chewing gum; and underpinning everything, the constant *clack-clack-clack* of one-clawed typing as harassed officers typed up statements.

Struggling against the tide of bodies, we made our way towards the interview rooms. Popping his head around a door, Dingus said a few words to someone inside.

'Okay, this one's yours,' he said, holding the door open. 'I'll be along the corridor.'

Crossing the threshold, I nodded at the officer standing against the wall. A few feet away a smooth voice said, 'Why, hello. We meet again.'

Sitting on the far side of a scratched desk, Lance Shoebury looked as nonplussed by proceedings as he had the night before. The only real difference was that now the flower in his buttonhole had wilted.

'Sleep well?' I asked.

'Not too badly, thanks,' he said, stretching his paws behind his head. 'I've slept in worse places.'

I didn't doubt it. 'I daresay you're wondering what you drove into last night.'

'It certainly wasn't the evening I'd anticipated,' he said, lighting a cigarette. 'But it was bound to happen sometime, you know. Those kind of places only last for so long before someone blows the whistle.' He smiled.

'You sound like you're speaking from experience.'

'Of course. Oh, look at that,' he said, suddenly noticing his wilting flower.

'Perhaps you'd care to tell me about it, Mr Shoebury.'

'Lance, please.' He blew smoke rings up at the ceiling. 'Well, what's to tell? I've been to a few similar establishments. Who hasn't? I don't see why it should be a big deal.'

I decided to take a punt. 'I don't suppose any of these other establishments were run by a guy called Falconetti, by any chance?'

He smiled again. 'Ah, I knew *you'd* know.' He raised his eyebrows suggestively. I didn't respond. 'Yes, Marvin Falconetti. Nice fella.'

'Not any more. His body was just found stuffed in a barrel up at Miss Bouchard's place.'

'Really? Oh dear. I hope she's not too upset.'

'We'd like to ask her about that, but nobody's seen her since the day before yesterday. Her place was gutted in a fire. They found Falconetti's body in the ruins.'

'Oh my goodness. You surely don't think *she* had anything to do with it? She's such a sweetheart.' He paused, frowned. 'Then again, she does have a bit of a temper.'

'Yeah?'

'This was a while ago you understand,' he said, tapping his cigarette into an ashtray. 'At one of Falconetti's places, when she was still just one of the girls – there was an argument between her and one of the others. Anyway, to cut a long story short, she started swinging this sock full of god knows what around and hit this poor girl on the side of the head with it; made a terrible noise when it struck. In the end Marvin had to drag Mimi off her before she could do any more damage. And Mimi didn't like *that*, let me tell you. But that was a one-off. It was a nice place, all told. One of the best. Actually, it was a real shame when it –'

'Burned down?' He let out a lungful of smoke. 'When did you next bump into her?'

'A couple of weeks ago. I'd just moved to town, and I heard about this new place from someone in a bar. Then he told me what you had to do just to get there. How could you not be intrigued? Anyway, Mimi was there but Falconetti wasn't and I didn't ask why. I just assumed they'd gone their separate ways.'

'Any thoughts as to where Mimi might have gone?'

'None. I never saw her outside of her... places of work.'

'The bar you mentioned – does it have a name?'

'Certainly does.' Thinking I'd misheard, I asked him to repeat it before writing it down. Then I asked him if it had a more formal name. He said it did and I wrote that down too.

Leaving Shoebury with the officer, I went back to Dingus's office to wait.

When he slouched in half an hour later, he looked like a crumpled-up brown paper bag.

'Well? How did it go with Chomsky?' I asked as he dropped into his chair.

'I don't know,' he said, massaging an ear. 'I just

don't know. Most of the time he just sat there with his arms folded saying nothing. On the few occasions he did talk it was to ask for a drink or a light for his cigarette.'

Despite what I'd just heard, I didn't change my opinion. 'He didn't do it, Dingus. I'm sure of that.'

'We'll see. Did you get anything out of Shoebury?'

'More than I'd hoped.' I told him about our chat, ending with the place of Falconetti's that'd burned down. 'Now either Mimi's very unlucky with the buildings she lives and works in, or –'

'– somebody close to her has a habit of torching them before anyone finds out what's going on in them. Only this time she's left two bodies behind.'

'Not to mention making herself homeless,' I added.

'Oh, I'm sure she must have somewhere else to go,' Dingus said. 'And perhaps we have someone here who could tell us where it is.' Picking up the phone, he spoke to the Desk Sergeant and asked him a question. 'Fifteen minutes ago? Good.' Smiling, he put the phone down. 'I think it's time we spoke to Miss Vincent, don't you?'

16.

Unlike Lance Shoebury who didn't seem to care that he was in a police station, Caro Vincent looked rather ill at ease, sitting bolt upright in her chair with her arms folded and legs crossed, staring at each of us in turn from behind her large spectacles.

'Okay, Miss Vincent,' Dingus began. 'Mimi Bouchard – where is she?'

'Miss Bouchard?' she said eventually in that buttoned-down way of hers. 'I've absolutely no idea.'

'Okay, let me put it another way. Where *might* she be? You see, she's not at home. But then again, neither is her home anymore. It was blown to kingdom come the night before last.' Widening her eyes, Vincent blinked a few times in response.

'You didn't hear about it? Why, the whole place went up like a Roman candle.' Another blink.

I decided to have a go. 'If you don't want to talk about where she is, perhaps you could tell us about the Salon.'

'Why? It's just a Salon.'

'*Just* a Salon? During daylight hours, perhaps. You see, me and the Lieutenant here paid it a visit last night. Now the downstairs part, the *real* Salon part, was empty.

But upstairs… upstairs doesn't look much like a Salon at all – in fact, it looks like it caters for a different type of clientele entirely.' Two blinks this time. 'I don't know about you Dingus, but I find Miss Vincent's loyalty to her boss rather touching. Unless it isn't loyalty, of course.'

'Maybe it's fear,' Dingus said, looking over at me.

'Could be. I mean, an Old Dog getting killed at a Pawnbroker's – a minor crime, surely – it's only an *Old* Dog, right? But it doesn't stop there. There's the body of one of Bouchard's goons we just found behind the Chomsky's place, not to mention the two bodies found up at what remains of her house. That's a lot of bodies. And with nobody else around to ask, it looks from here like you're carrying the can. Given all that, I think I'd be pretty scared.'

Suddenly Vincent was leaning forward, arms and legs uncrossed, paws on the top of the table, claws scratching the surface. 'What do you mean, *two* bodies?' she said, staring at us in turn.

Dingus and I exchanged glances. 'There were two bodies found at the property. One outside, and the other in a barrel in the basement where she grew enough dope to keep a forest full of Squirrels high for a fortnight.'

Her claws weren't just scratching the table now – they were embedded in its surface. 'In a barrel,' she whispered. 'In the basement...'

It was like we weren't there – she kept saying the words over and over to herself, her paws closing into fists despite her claws being stuck in the table, causing it to wobble madly before the claws eventually broke free of the surface, just as it looked like the table was about to be raised off the floor. Staring down at them, she flexed them repeatedly, a strange light coming into her eyes.

What she did next only took a few seconds. Producing one of the Salon's business cards from her jacket, she placed it carefully on the table blank side up, then pierced the pad on her left paw with a claw from her right, causing a thick globule of blood to bloom around it. Pulling the claw free of the pad, she quickly scratched three bloodied initials across the back of the card before picking it up, tearing it into strips and shoving the pieces into her mouth.

Hypnotised by the awfulness of what we were seeing, it wasn't until she started to choke on the bits of card that either of us reacted. Running around the table, Dingus started slapping her on the back. 'Get the Doctor in here, quick!' Dingus shouted to the officer at the back of the room.

As Vincent was being led away by the Doctor minus the mushed-up business card and the contents of her stomach, the Lieutenant asked: 'What did she write on the card?'

'The letters W, K and Y,' I told him. 'Presumably Wareham, Krukowski and Yang, that property firm I told you about who seem to be representing Miss Bouchard. I've been meaning to pay them a visit, but things like dead bodies keep getting in the way.'

'I think now might be as good a time as any, Benji,' Dingus said, rising from his chair.

17.

The offices of Wareham, Krukowski & Yang were tucked away in an anonymous side street, among other similar businesses. Looking in their windows, we saw a succession of bored-looking animals in shabby suits surrounded by paper. But in the office third from the end of the row, not even the lights were on.

Knocking the front door for a few minutes, Dingus got no response. After that he tried the handle; surprisingly, the door wasn't locked. Stepping into the small lobby he tried the main door, but it was. After ringing the buzzer and knocking a few times, he gave up.

'Let's try round the back,' he said.

Heading along the street to the end of the row, a light rain began to fall. To the left was a narrow alleyway, sloping down to the rear of the buildings. By the time we got there the rain had become heavy.

The door we wanted was at the top of half a dozen grey stone steps, each turning progressively darker as the rain hit them. Then I noticed the top step, which was darker than any of them. On it was a sticky-looking stain, which seemed to be coming from under the door. As it mixed with the rain it became lighter in colour, thinning out to a thin pink drool which threatened to drop onto the step below.

Dingus and I looked at each other, then we climbed the steps.

Trying the door even though chances were there was a body slumped against it even if it wasn't locked, it nonetheless began to ease inwards, revealing nothing but a substantial pool of congealed blood on the floor. Stepping across it we went inside, closing the door against the rain. It too was covered in blood.

'Looks like they shot whoever it was up against the door,' Dingus said.

'Then they picked up the body and carried it down the steps. Presumably to a waiting car.'

'Mimi?'

'If it was she had help lifting the body.'

Dingus squinted up at me. 'Vincent –?'

Before waiting for an answer, the Lieutenant scurried off, looking for a phone.

While he searched I took a look around what turned out to be the kitchen. A grimy coffee pot sat on a metal draining board next to a sink filled with dirty cups. A few feet away, a battered old table leaned against the wall, on which were half-a-dozen scrunched-up food wrappers and an ashtray containing so much ash it looked like someone had cremated several small rodents. Next door was home to a number of large grey file cabinets, all forced open. One of them was empty; a little card tucked into the metal pocket at the front of the drawer bore the legend MB PROPERTIES. Rifling through the other cabinets, I couldn't find a single transaction that had occurred since The Terror. The whole outfit had 'Front Organisation' written all over it.

Going through to the office, where Dingus was chatting away on the phone, I stopped at the first desk and looked at a dusty framed photograph standing next to the typewriter. The photo was of three Sappy's, two guys and a mysterious-looking dame, standing under an umbrella out at the front of the building: presumably the original Wareham, Krukowski, and Yang. As always when I saw pictures of Humans I found myself wondering what had become of them, and if it was one of their pets that was running this shabby office; and if it was their blood that was decorating the back door. The desk had six drawers, three on either side of the seat. Sitting down, I began trying them. Four contained nothing more interesting than used and unused stationary and empty scotch bottles; the other two were locked. Forcing the first one I found a stack of magazines, the kind that would've made the Mouse blush for a week; and in the second I found paper – lots and lots of paper, listing the properties that Wareham, Krukowski & Yang were involved with – Mimi's Salon, her house – and all the houses on Sebald Street. And, at the back of the pile was a document listing Wareham, Krukowski & Yang's Board of Directors: Donny Wareham, Marvin Falconetti – and Mimi Bouchard.

'Well, whaddya know…'

Hanging up the phone, Dingus came over. 'Found something?'

'It looks like whoever it was came here looking for files and didn't get them,' I said. 'Or Wareham made copies. Look.' I handed him the pile of papers.

'So Wareham, Krukowski & Yang weren't Wareham, Krukowski & Yang at all – they were Wareham, Falconetti & Bouchard,' Dingus muttered, taking a look through. 'But they used the old company name so no-one would know Mimi was involved.'

'Yup. And with Falconetti out of the way – not that anyone *knows* he's out of the way – and presumably now Wareham, she's in sole charge.'

'But if we buy the idea that it was Mimi who died in the fire, then we're supposed to believe that Falconetti's still in charge because nobody knows he's dead.' He clutched the sides of his skull. 'Does your head hurt as much as mine does?'

'More. What news of Vincent? You were on the phone a while.'

'She's back in the interview room, waiting for us. Apparently after we left she calmed right down. The doc had a look at her and told her to get some rest but she insisted that she had to speak to us – said she wanted to apologise for her behaviour and would explain everything when we got back. Anyway, there's an officer in the room with her and I've told him to keep an eye on her, just in case.'

It seemed to take a long time for the lab boys to arrive; when they did, Dingus explained things as quickly as he could. Then we hightailed it back to the station.

Miss Vincent had a story to tell.

18.

Despite assurances to the contrary, when we got to the station I half expected to see her gnawing away on a phone directory or something. Instead she just sat there, quite still; a little subdued, but definitely with us.

'I'm sorry about earlier,' she said. 'It was such a shock, finding out like that.' I gave her a blank look; so did Dingus. 'The body in the barrel – it was Falconetti, wasn't it?'

'Yes,' Dingus said. 'Were you and he –?' Vincent nodded.

'Tell us about it.'

'We met in a Salon I was working at,' she began. 'He came in with one of his girls. Of course, I didn't know what he was involved in then, innocent that I was.' She smiled. 'I figured I must've been doing something right though because he repeatedly returned with different girls. Then one day he came alone. I was plain – I knew that – but still he kept coming... soon we were –' she broke off, staring at the ceiling behind our heads for a second.

'By the time he took me to one of his clubs, I knew how he paid the bills. But I found I didn't much care. It was at the club that I saw Mimi for the first time.'

Picking up the glass of water beside her, she took a drink and set it back down. 'I thought she was just another girl at first, although one with a bit more jewellery than the others. I liked her. She took me under her wing, like a sister. She used to take me out shopping for clothes.' She smiled at the memory. 'After a while I realised she liked Marv too, but not in the same way I did – she liked him because of what he could do for her.

'It wasn't long before she was practically running the club, and Marv was away a lot on business, so we saw less and less of each other. Then one day he left town for good. I thought he'd got tired of me. Mimi told me that he was setting up other clubs across the country and that he wouldn't be back. Anyway, I was devastated. Then she did the most amazing thing: she asked me if I wanted to be manageress of a new Salon on Montcrieff Terrace. She knew I wanted my own place – and yes, I knew what would be going on upstairs in the evenings – but again, I didn't care; it was a dream fulfilled.' She shook her head sadly.

'A couple of days later Mimi invited me up to her place for drinks, to sort out the details. I was a bit nervous – was I really up to it? I didn't want to let her down. I was also missing Marv terribly. When I told her all this she poured me a drink, put her arm round me, smiled and said, "You don't need him, hon – you don't need anybody. And you won't let me down – I have every confidence in you. Why, running that Salon'll be like shooting fish in a barrel." And all the time he was up there at the house, beneath our feet, in a barrel of his own,' she finished, her voice dead.

When she spoke next it was to ask for a cigarette. Taking one from the officer at the back of the room, she took a few drags and tried to compose herself.

'Tell us about Wareham, Krukowski and Yang,' Dingus said eventually.

'The minute you showed up she realised it was all going wrong, that you'd figure out what was happening,' she continued, looking at me. 'But Mimi said she knew exactly what to do. She said – she said she was going to burn her house down.'

Vincent looked stunned for a second. 'It sounded crazy, but once she started to explain it to me, it made sense. It would get rid of a lot of evidence, and it would take the heat off the Salon for a while, which I was to continue to run as normal. She also said that it'd all be done in such a way that everyone would think she'd died in the fire. Oh boy.' Letting out a long drag of smoke, she went quiet for a while.

'What about when attention focused back on the Salon?' Dingus asked.

'I was to plead ignorance. I didn't have keys for the other floors and as far as I was concerned the building was shut up tight from when I went home until the next morning. But before that she wanted me to do something for her: get all the files from Donny Wareham.

'Wareham had been by the Salon a few times to see Mimi, and was sweet on me. Well, anything with fur, really. She arranged for me to meet him at his office. One of Mimi's thugs, Hagen, would drive me there and wait outside. I was to try and get the files from him without any trouble; if that didn't work, Hagen would come in and threaten him. It was working out fine until Hagen got impatient and blundered in. Wareham got mad at him and there was a struggle and –' she sucked on the cigarette for a second, took a sip of water.

'After that I was in shock. Hagen moved the body away from the door and I went and sat in the car. He stayed inside, looking for the files. When he came out he threw a folder in the back seat and told me to open the trunk. He brought the body out, slung over his shoulder, and stuck it in the trunk; said he was going to dump the body up at the house as close to the fire as possible, so the police would think it was someone who lived there.

'The fire was already raging by the time we got there. He managed to get close enough so the body would get burned up in the blaze. Then he drove me home and told me to keep my mouth shut. After that it was just a case of waiting until you showed up and for Mimi to get in touch.'

'Who set the fire?' Dingus asked.

'Dash Norman, I imagine – he did a few jobs like that for Marv in the past. One time he blew up a building but didn't get far enough away before it exploded. Ended up as deaf as a post. But he was useful to have around, so he was kept on as a gardener.'

'Only it wasn't just roses he was cultivating.'

She gave a small smile. 'Ah, yes. They've been a very profitable side-line for Mimi, those plants. You can never have enough jewellery or plants, she used to tell me. Even if they never saw the daylight...' For the briefest of moments the strange light we'd seen earlier came back into her eyes.

'Did she keep anything else of interest up there?' I asked.

'Hmm? If she did I didn't know about it. It was just home I think – the nearest thing she had to one anyway.'

'But presumably she must have somewhere else to go,' Dingus said. 'You don't blow up your house unless you have somewhere else to stay.'

'True,' she said. 'But I don't know where it could be.'

'What about associates we might try?' I suggested.

'You must've heard a lot of names bandied about. Anything at all.'

'Well,' she mused. 'Certain names did crop up more than once, but I've no idea in relation to what.'

'Such as?'

'Well, she did mention the Barrett brothers on Belmont Avenue a couple of time. They run some kind of bootleg hooch operation.'

'Belmont Avenue?' It took me a second or two to recall where I'd heard the name before. 'Same street as the soup kitchen?'

'That's it. Mimi was interested in getting into the liquor trade.'

'Any others?'

'Leary Way. I think that's what it was called. I heard her mention it on the phone several times but when she saw me she'd lower her voice so I can't be sure about it. Janklow's – that was another.' She took a sip of water. 'Hmm. What else? Quesnay's, someone called Bingham, someone called Osterlein... there was the Relf or Ralf partnership... yeah, Relf or Ralf. Or Relf. Um... Relf or...' scribbling away, I'd just caught up and was about to ask her which it was – Relf or Ralf – when Dingus put a paw on my arm. Looking over at him, he nodded at Vincent. Following his gaze, I saw Vincent staring straight past us, that strange light in her eyes once more, her mouth moving silently, paws shaking on top of the table.

'Miss Vincent?' Dingus said gently. 'Are you okay?'

It took a second or two for her eyes to slide back towards us. 'Hmm?'

'You were telling us about Miss Bouchard's associates.'

'I was? Well, I can give you names, but I've no idea what use they'd be. But I'll tell you what *is* interesting –

what she grows in her basement.' She grinned madly, her claws drumming on the table. 'Do you know about that?'

Dingus and I exchanged glances. 'We know about that, Miss Vincent. But –'

'And it isn't just the customers who smoke that stuff either – the girls do too – at a discounted cost, of course. Mimi says it helps keep them in line. And Dash, he uses it, but he says he only does it to see if it's ready or not.' She cackled at that. 'But Hagen and Moseley, they don't use it – oh no, not them.' Now her claws were practically skittering across the table.

'And what about you, Miss Vincent? You ever tried it?'

'*Me*?' she tried to look shocked. 'Me? Never.'

'You sure?' I asked. 'It might help explain your erratic behaviour since you got here.'

'Now,' she said, waving a shaky paw in our faces, 'you're just being offensive. Now: names. You wanted names. Well, there's… um…'

For a few minutes we lost her completely, and Dingus told the officer at the back of the room to fetch the 'doc again. During that time we learned nothing about Mimi Bouchard but a lot about Caro Vincent as she painfully unravelled before our eyes. When she was finally led out of the room into an ambulance she had a blanket wrapped around her and was shivering uncontrollably, despite the stuffiness in the interview room. Lighting a cigar, Dingus shook his head sadly.

'What do you think will happen to her?' I asked.

'They'll take her to the hospital and do the best they can for her. The thing is, nobody knows exactly what that is anymore.' He took a lung-busting pull on his cigar. 'You see how quickly that came on her, that change? I've heard of that happening before. Sometime it just happens once; other times they stay like that, not fit for anything. God knows why they take it – I mean, nobody knows *what* effect these things have on us, do they? Take liquor for example – how come Dogs can drink it but Cats can't? It's a mystery. I'll have someone outside her room, on the off-chance she'll be fit to answer questions at some point. But I'm not hopeful.'

'If nothing else we know for certain now that Chomsky didn't torch Mimi's pad,' I said, trying to be positive.

'Yeah. But he still needs to tell us what happened with Moseley.'

'If anything *did* happen with Moseley, and I don't believe it did.'

'In that case, he should say so.'

'Maybe he will, now he's been subjected to the lousy coffee in here for a few hours.'

'Well, let's go see. Who knows, with you there he might even break into a sentence.'

When we entered the interview room he ignored Dingus and turned his attention to me. 'Hey Spriteman,' he snapped. 'You find who killed Gino yet?'

He appeared a little nervier than the last time I saw him, the cut above his eye livid under the sharp bright lights.

'You seemed to think it was Moseley before. The Lieutenant here tells me you're not being very cooperative.'

'What the hell does he expect? Dragging me down here and asking me a lot of damn fool questions.'

'You came quite willingly as I remember it, Mr Chomsky. And it's just one question: whether you killed Moseley or not.'

He didn't speak for maybe a minute. Then he sighed heavily. 'Okay; okay. You want to know the truth? Well, the truth is this: I don't know if I killed him or not. I remember being in Kowalski's and I remember Spriteman taking me home and after that I don't remember anything until the morning when I woke up with a splitting head and a cut above my eye. I must've blacked out or something. And you know what? It's a damned shame.'

I frowned at him. 'A shame?'

'Yeah, a shame – because if I did have the guts to off that old bastard I've no memory of doing it.'

To say I was taken aback is putting it mildly; not so much by what he said but the vehemence with which he said it.

'Benji?' Dingus was tugging at my arm. 'Come on. I think you should go now.'

Out in the corridor I didn't know what to think. Could he have done it?

As I stood there, Dingus said something to me, but I was barely aware of what it was. Trying to reason it through, I decided that if nothing else at least with Dingus Chomsky was in safe hands; I could do nothing for him at the moment. Only I could; I could do the job I was supposed to be getting paid for, namely finding out who killed his brother.

I could try, anyway.

19.

Before I began, I decided to give the Mouse a call to see what – if anything – he'd turned up. Using a pay phone at the station, I was a bit surprised when I got no response from the office. Then I looked at my watch: it was after six thirty. Phoning the Spayley residence, I spoke to one of his siblings who said he hadn't seen him since he came home earlier in the day "smelling all funny". After taking a bath, he'd gone back out again.

'But he did phone a few hours ago with a message for you,' his brother, one of nine, informed me. 'Because he said you might call. He made me write it down.' After rustling a sheet of paper and clearing his throat, he began to read the message.

'"One: Regarding Chomsky's movements yesterday – no discrepancy. On leaving Mr S, Chomsky drove to Roly's, a bar on 24th Street before eventually ordering a taxi to take him back to Moncrieff Terrace, the driver describing him as 'drunk as a Lord'. From there he went into Kowalski's bar, remaining until Mr S took him home. Two: Spoke to Sadie the Goat – nothing unusual heard. Three: Tried to contact Harvey, but not at home."'

'And Linus called you a few hours ago with all this?' I interrupted. 'Did he say where he was going?'

'Yeah, he did.' Again, the rustle of paper. '"Four: Going to the forest to try out a theory with the potential to significantly change the case."'

'It seems to be taking him a while,' I remarked.

'I was thinking the same thing, Mr Spriteman. If he ever thinks he's going to be late back he says so. He's particular like that.'

He certainly was. Thanking his brother, I rung off and headed out to the forest, wondering what on earth it was the Mouse thought he'd find there that was so important. And why was it taking so long? The Mouse – all 240 pounds of him – had the constitution of an Ox; but if it meant putting his 'theory' to a forest full of hundreds of stoned and angry Squirrels – not to mention the Bull – then I didn't much fancy his chances.

Driving through the trees with the window down, it took me several minutes before I realised that the smell had gone. Night was drawing in and the forest was still. Taking the roads slowly, I saw nobody; not even any Old animals.

Eventually spotting the Mouse's car parked in a lay-by at the side of the road, I pulled in behind it and closed my car door quietly, the stillness in the forest grating on my nerves. Taking a deep breath, I forced myself to go into the woods.

I got maybe five paces in when I heard someone giggling nearby.

'Who's there?' More giggling. Moving slowly towards it, it stopped suddenly, so I did the same. Flicking on my flashlight I swept it around, but saw nothing. Taking another few steps, twigs cracked beneath my shoes, and the giggling started again. A few more steps, and I was almost on top of the source; or rather, beneath it. Shining my flashlight up into the nearest tree, the beam picked out several Squirrels sitting in a line along a branch, shielding their eyes against the glare with their tiny paws.

'Hey, turn that light out, can't you?' one of them squeaked.

'Sorry to disturb the party,' I said, switching the flashlight off. 'I'm looking for someone. A large white Mouse. His car's back there.'

'Anyone seen a Mouse up here?' a second voice said.

'I can't see one,' someone else mumbled amid a rustle of leaves.

'Hey, maybe he's hiding,' a fourth voice suggested, a strange mixture of drawl and squeak. 'Let's go take a look.'

For maybe a minute the branches above me were alive with activity. Then: 'Nope, he's not around here,' the drawling voice said. 'He must be on a higher branch. What's he wearing?'

'A pink Elephant costume,' I said. 'So long, fellas.'

'Well, I like *that*,' someone muttered as I walked away.

With their chittering fading into the distance behind me, I became aware once more of the silence and darkness of the forest. Then, as I went to flick the flashlight back on, I was reminded of what the first Squirrel had said to me: *Hey, turn that light out, can't you?* It took me a second to realise why it made me feel uncomfortable, and then I remembered: it was the exact same phrase I'd heard when I saw that Tuke silhouetted against that staircase a week or two earlier. Suddenly I was back there, watching that huge shadow beak stabbing, *lunging* at something I couldn't see. My heart thumped heavily in my chest at what felt like some dire kind of warning; then as if in response, I heard groaning ahead of me.

My pulse quickened. The same could not be said for my feet. Switching on the flashlight as I dragged my heels, I heard another groan. Then in a gap between the trees I saw the Mouse standing with his back to me, his large pink ears almost translucent in the beam from the flashlight. There was a further groan, then another, both at ground level. Pointing the light downwards, it picked out half a dozen Squirrels standing beside a tree, holding their heads. Then the Mouse turned round.

'Mr S?' he said, squinting into the light.

'Linus? Are you okay?'

'Better after having a long soak in the tub,' he said. 'Still a bit light-headed though, for some reason. Did Lucius give you my message?'

As he spoke, I noticed he was cradling something wrapped in a small blanket. When I shone my light at it, it groaned.

'Who's in the blanket?' I asked.

'Lower the light and I'll show you.' Opening the blanket a little, I looked inside. Resting in the crook of the Mouse's arm was something that looked like a rat-faced baby, screwing itself into a ball and moaning.

'I can't get any sense out of any of them,' the Mouse said, looking down at it and the others around him. 'This one said he was cold, so I got him a blanket from my car. But the others... half of them say they want to die while the other half can't stop laughing. I don't know what to do.'

'Oh, it's probably just some strange forest virus,' I said feebly. 'But never mind that – what are *you* doing out here?'

'Oh, it was this dumb idea I had,' he said irritably. 'Something that Medical Examiner said earlier, about

Moseley being punched. I'm no Clancy Mr S, but didn't it strike you that punch was a bit low?'

With the body laid out on the ground it was hard to tell, but it was possible. 'What about it?'

'Well... I wondered if maybe it wasn't a punch at all, but a butt?'

'A butt?'

'Yeah, you know. Like this.' Lowering his head, the Mouse ran a few steps towards the nearest tree, the Squirrel in his arms protesting as he was jostled about. 'I got to thinking maybe the Bull had done it – they dip their heads like that to attack. Suppose he and the Squirrels had ambushed Moseley in the woods, stopping his car like they had Hagen's – only this time they got him *out* of the car? But before they could finish him off, Moseley managed to get back inside and drive off. It'd explain the low blow, plus he'd have been in pretty bad shape by the time he reached Montcrieff Terrace. And then I had another thought: what if a few of the Squizzes, armed with the shards of glass that were stuck in the trees following the explosion, managed to hitch a ride on top of Moseley's car as he drove away? Then, when he parked the car they swarmed all over him and cut his throat.'

He stopped, looked embarrassed. 'It wasn't 'til I'd got here that I realised how stupid it all sounded – the blow was far too low for a start, and even if it hadn't been, where were the puncture wounds from the Bull's horns? The Coroner never mentioned any. And as for the Squirrels and the glass –' he shook his head sadly. 'I don't know Mr S, I guess I'm just not thinking straight lately – I still feel a bit woozy from this morning. Maybe I'm coming down with what these guys have got. Anyway, I thought while I was here I'd try and get some information from them, but as you can see –'

Evidently catching the realisation on my face he stopped. 'Mr S? What is it?'

For a while I couldn't speak. Instead I just stared at him as the implications sunk in. 'Linus,' I said, 'you're a genius. But I wish to hell you weren't.'

The Mouse looked hurt. 'I already said it was a dumb idea, Mr S. There's no need to make fun of me.'

'I'm not making fun of you,' I said. 'In fact, you're on the right lines.'

His eyes widened. 'I am?'

I nodded. 'But you've got all the details wrong – the weapon, the location – even the animals.'

'I have? Then who killed him?'

When I told him, the Mouse's face somehow grew even whiter. Raising his paws to his whiskers in horror, he lost his grip on the bundle in his arms and it fell to the forest floor.

'Ouch,' said the Squirrel.

20.

Forty minutes or so later I was parking my car in Montcrieff Terrace, the Mouse pulling up behind me just after. When Sascha opened the door to us she looked even worse than she had that morning, knitting her paws together frantically, and the odour of soap I'd noticed before was now overpowering. But as strong as it was, it wasn't enough to mask another smell coming from inside, a smell that I thought I recognised.

'Come on through,' Sascha told us, leading us through the shop towards the living room. 'We – we were hoping it would be you and not –' her words trailed off. Inside, I saw I was right about the smell. Standing beside the coffee table with her head slightly bowed, Sadie looked almost as wretched as Sascha did. Next to her on the table was a small glass with a straw in it.

'How's Willard?' Sadie asked.

'Oh, he's making his presence felt,' I said, picking up the glass. At the bottom was a thin, chalky residue. 'How's the headache?'

'It doesn't seem to be getting any better,' Sadie said, her eyes not meeting mine.

'That's because you need to drain the glass,' the Mouse said. 'Most of the tablet's stuck at the bottom. But you can't get to it because the angle's wrong. Here, let me help.' Taking the glass off me, he put it to her mouth and tilted it. I don't know why, but watching the Mouse hold the glass steady while Sadie sucked the last of the pill up the straw was one of the saddest things I've ever seen in my life.

While this was going on, Sascha, as was her wont, was in the kitchen making coffee. Reappearing with a tray, the crockery on it rattled madly in her shaking paws. Taking it from her I put it on the table, poured the coffee and waited for them to talk.

We didn't have to wait long. 'If only I'd answered the phone yesterday lunchtime when you called,' Sascha said, looking at the Mouse and rubbing her paws furiously, 'maybe none of this would have happened. He always has to get to the phone before me – it's like some stupid game with him. Anyway, when he put it down he was grinning from ear to ear. I asked what had happened but before he could explain he said he'd seen your secretary out in the street and went after her. A second or two later he came back, grabbed the car keys and left without saying a word. When it started to get dark and there was still no sign of him I began to get worried. After a while I couldn't stand it so I phoned Sadie.'

'Phoned –?' the Mouse asked, startled.

'I've worked out a way to use it,' Sadie told him. 'I sometimes lose the connection getting it off the hook and dialling out's a nuisance, but mostly it's fine. Anyhow, I said he was probably just out drinking –'

'– And I said Willard didn't drink any more, not after the last time,' Sascha interrupted. 'We always end up having a row. So he promised me: *no more drinking.*' Spitting out these last few words, she folded her arms tight across her chest.

Then, following on from what I thought had happened to Moseley I had another little eureka moment, recalling her flash of anger in my office.

'That's how he got the cut above his eye,' I said, my voice hushed. 'You hit him, didn't you?'

For a few seconds she couldn't speak, worried her paws even harder. 'Sometimes, when he goes too far,' she said, her voice as tight as a drum, 'I lose my temper.'

'I said she should go over to Kowalski's and check anyway,' Sadie said, hurriedly bringing it back to the topic at hand. 'But she wouldn't do it.'

'Since what happened to Gino I don't like to go out after dark,' Sascha stated. 'I don't feel safe any more. And it wasn't fair to ask Sadie.' If the look on her face was anything to go by, I doubt she'd have gone anyway.

'By now I was as annoyed as I was worried but I was determined not to let him get to me, so I kept myself busy doing paperwork. Then I heard noise out in the street and that's when I saw you.'

'What happened after I helped you put him to bed? I'm guessing he didn't stay there.'

'When you left, I called Sadie to tell her he was back. I hung up the phone and heard all this noise upstairs. When I got up there I found him clattering around in the hall. He said he had something to tell me. I told him I didn't want to hear it, that it could wait until the morning when he was sober. But he said he had to tell me now, and he told me about the fire at that – that *creature's* house, and about how it was time she got what was coming to her. Then he said he wasn't tired any more, and that we should celebrate.

'I tried to get him back to bed but he wouldn't go. He went downstairs to get a drink. Then he remembered that the only alcohol we have in the house now is sherry, so he said he was going back to Kowalski's for a real drink. He started walking towards the door, and I reached out to stop him. When he shook me off, he used a word worse than any I've ever heard him use before and that's when I saw red – I lashed out and one of my claws caught him above the eye. And it – drew blood.'

Sobbing, she put her paws up to her face, and for the first time I got a good look at them; some of the fur was missing because of all the rubbing, leaving them raw. A couple of the claws were broken and one was missing.

Rushing to the kitchen, the Mouse got her a glass of water and gave her his handkerchief. After taking a gulp of water and blowing her nose noisily, she carried on.

'Neither of us said anything. We just stood facing each other. After a while, he turned and went to bed. Eventually I went up myself but despite being exhausted I couldn't sleep. I just lay there for ages, tossing and turning. And that's when I heard someone clattering about outside.

'Willard was fast asleep by then – I could hear him snoring through the wall – but I couldn't have gone in there anyway, not after what had just happened. So I got up and went to the window, and in the moonlight I saw that disgusting old Dog in the yard, the one Willard said had killed Gino. And he must've seen the curtain move, because as I was watching him he looked straight up and saw me.' She began to worry her paws again.

'I was terrified – I knew that if I called the police, by the time they got here it would be too late, so I called Sadie. But by the time she answered, he was battering the door, trying to get in.'

'What did you do?' I asked Sadie.

'I dropped the phone, eventually got my back door open and saw him trying to break in. For a moment or two I was frozen with fear then something else took over, and I ran towards the Chomsky's. The gate was wide open so I charged at him. I was maybe a couple of feet away when he heard me and turned round. I sprang at him and I caught him in the gut, and he landed back against Sascha's door.'

'There was a tremendous thud and I heard him groaning,' Sascha carried on. 'At first I thought he must've injured himself trying to break the door down. But when he started swearing, using the most vile language I'd ever heard, I realised Sadie must be out there. And all I could think was: *he's going to kill her.* Then it was like it'd been with Willard earlier, everything in a red mist. I got the back door open and saw him hobbling towards Sadie and ran, and my claws were swiping at his throat and there was all this blood –' Stopping again for a few seconds, she took a deep breath.

'Despite everything we'd done he managed to stay on his feet. But now instead of coming towards us he started to stumble away. So we both ran inside and I bolted the door.'

'Then what happened?'

'Sadie wanted to call the police, but I managed to talk her out of it. If they hadn't taken what happened to Gino seriously, what would they make of this? We thought he'd be long gone by the time they arrived. Besides, I'm not sure I could've opened the door to anyone at that point.'

I turned to Sadie. 'So you didn't go home?'

'I didn't want to be alone. I don't think I'd have made it anyway – my head was splitting. I went into the living room and lay down on the floor and the room started spinning. The next thing I remember is Sascha shaking me awake the next morning.'

'What did you do?' I asked Sascha.

'I didn't think he'd be back, but I put the kitchen table and chairs against the back door. Then I went into the living room. I sat there for a long time, listening for any stray noise. I was sure I wouldn't sleep, but at some point I must have, because the next thing I remember is light coming through the curtains. I guess I was exhausted. When Sadie woke up I eventually moved all the furniture from the back door. Then maybe an hour or so after Sadie went home I got up the nerve to go out and put some stuff in the trash. And that's when I saw him, perhaps ten feet from where he'd been last night, wedged in among the garbage like he'd crawled in there to die. And I didn't know what to do – I couldn't call the police because they'd have wanted to know why I hadn't called last night, and Sadie had a headache and Willard was still asleep, so I called you, and –'

After that, Sascha was inconsolable. Sadie and the Mouse did their best with her, but to no real end. For my part, I tried to distract myself by wondering how the hell we were going to get a Goat up to the police station.

In the end, we took the back seats out of my car so Sadie could stand up, the Mouse holding onto her when the road got bumpy. Sascha sat in the front next to me.

For the duration of the journey, nobody spoke.

21.

Judging by the looks we got, it seemed a safe bet they'd never had a Goat in the station before. Not that Sadie noticed; she seemed shell-shocked with it all. Beside her, Sascha worried at her paws, twisting and turning them over and over like she was washing with an invisible bar of soap.

Going to the front desk I exchanged a few words with the Desk Sergeant, a perpetually weary but decent German Shepherd who nodded before looking over at the traumatised creatures the Mouse and I had brought in.

'Leave them with me,' he said with a wink as he picked up the phone, 'I'll make sure they're all right.' Seconds later I heard a voice come through his earpiece. 'Lieutenant says to go on through.'

The Mouse looked at me, unsure what to do next. I thought about it, and a germ of an idea came to me. 'Hang around until I've spoken to Dingus,' I told him. 'Go grab yourself a drink.' Hating being idle, he reluctantly slouched off towards the canteen while I went to see the Lieutenant.

'Well, that explains Chomsky's attitude since he arrived,' Dingus said once I'd filled him in. 'How are the two ladies' doing?'

'Not good,' I told him.

'Okay, I'll leave them for the minute. Let's see what Chomsky has to say instead.'

'*What?*' he yelled. 'Sascha and Sadie? You're crazy, both of you.'

'Look, we understand why you've been covering up for them,' I said. 'But they explained what happened. They explained *everything*.'

For the briefest of moments he seemed stunned, raising a paw up to the cut above his eye before stopping himself.

'Boy, I never heard such a load of crap. From him, I expect it –' he jerked his cigarette in the Lieutenant's general direction. 'But *you*, Spriteman –' shaking his head in disgust, he stared down at the desk. Then, after extinguishing what was left of his cigarette in the ashtray, he looked up.

'Okay,' he sighed. 'Okay. I see what you're trying to do. I've been holding out on you, so you tell me you're going to pin it on them to hurry me along. I understand that. Fine. You win. I admit it – it was me. I croaked the old bastard. Satisfied? Now, let them go. This is no place for them.'

'How did you do it?' Dingus asked.

'I don't know! I've told you all this. I was so drunk I don't remember. What does it matter anyway? *I've confessed*, haven't I?'

'But you can't tell us how you did it,' Dingus said patiently. 'Whereas Sascha and Sadie have given Mr Spriteman here a detailed account which seems to fit. So unless you can come up with something more concrete…' Leaving the sentence hanging, Dingus headed for the door with me behind him.

'But, I *confessed*, dammit!' Chomsky shrieked. 'Hey – don't you walk out on me!' When we didn't respond, he cranked up the volume and the insults a couple of notches.

'*I know animals, you know – you don't know who you're messing with you mangy bastards, I'll have you turned into chopped liver! Come* back *here! I'll have your nuts in a noose you pair of furry motherf–*' at which point Dingus slammed the door shut behind us.

'I think we'll keep him here for a while,' Dingus said in the corridor, rubbing a paw across his lined face. 'Until I've had the story off the ladies' first hand. Maybe he'll have calmed down a bit by then. Speaking of which, maybe it'd be better if I spoke to Sascha and Sadie sooner rather than later.'

'Maybe so,' I agreed. 'Hey, why not take the Mouse in with you? You know the soothing effect he seems to have on the female population. And he's always telling me how he'd love to sit in on a police interview.'

For a second I thought he was going to say no, at which point I'd have thrown my chat with Lance Shoebury in his face. But instead he said, 'You know, that's not a bad idea. Okay, send him along.' Smiling, I did as I was told.

Finding the Mouse sulking over a glass of milk in the canteen, I gave him the good news. Barely able to contain himself, he emptied the glass and jumped up from his chair.

'Thanks, Mr S,' he grinned. 'But what about you? You're going after Mimi, right? Won't you need some help?'

'Um, no, I'll be fine,' I assured him. 'You stay here and help out the Lieutenant. He's got a lot on his plate. It'll be good experience for you.' Happy with my explanation, he trotted over to the interview room. Equally happy, I headed out to my car and drove back to the office.

Despite the hour, a few yellow rectangles of light from the building across the street stood out against the night sky, a foolhardy few burning the midnight oil; but in the building which housed my office, the only lights still on were those on either side of the elevator. Inside it, I pushed a button and not for the first time took a long look at the feline staring back at me in the mirrored glass. After some consideration, I decided he didn't look too bad.

On the fourth floor, my shoes echoed in the corridor. A couple of offices before my own, weak light spilled under a door on the left and I heard what sounded like someone murmuring sweet nothings, presumably into a telephone. Unlocking the door second from the end on the right, I walked through the anteroom and into my office. Parking myself in my chair, I clicked on the small angle-poise lamp on my desk and started to reach for the telephone before changing my mind; at this time of night, I knew *exactly* where the Rabbit would be. So instead, sighing a long, sorry sigh, I swivelled my chair to the right and wheeled myself over to the lanky, large-leaved plant that seemed to survive on nothing but the coffee grounds I tipped into its pot each day, and the picture hanging above it on the wall. It wasn't a particularly interesting picture; just some dull-looking flowers in a drab-coloured vase. But I hadn't picked it to be interesting; I'd picked it because it was cheap, and because it was the kind of picture you wouldn't give a second glance to. Standing up, I took the picture off the wall and looked at the small, square metal door that was behind it, or more specifically, at the small dial in its centre. Turning the dial it made a noise like amplified crickets until the tumblers clicked; then the door gently swung open.

The irony was that I got a safe after seeing first hand how useless they were against the wrong animal –

in this case, a gang of vicious Moles. Until the start of the year I'd managed perfectly well without one, trusting my most precious belongings to a nook under the loose floorboards beneath my desk. But in the end, figuring that with three floors between me and *terra firma* and with the Moles now behind bars, I should fork out the necessary cash.

Inside were the usual bundles of files and legal documents that safes were made for, but on top was the thing I wanted – or rather didn't. Taking it out, I briefly looked down at the cold, weighty object in my paw before sliding it into my jacket pocket.

I don't like guns. If I can avoid using one – hell, avoid *carrying* one – I will. But the way the case was going I figured it might be better if I had it with me, if only as a last resort. I tried to kid myself this was the real reason I didn't want the Mouse around, telling myself that he'd been through enough lately after inhaling all that smoke. But deep down I knew it wasn't true: the truth was that I wanted to find Mimi myself, try and make amends for all those wasted months.

Locking the safe door, I put the picture back in place and turned to my desk, looked at the card game I'd started the day before. Sweeping the cards into a drawer, I took a deep breath. I had my gun and I had a list of leads from Vincent. All I needed now was to see where they both took me.

Snapping off the angle-poise lamp, I marched out of the office.

22.

The first two leads I checked led nowhere. From the front, the Barrett Brothers' Dry Goods Emporium seemed perfectly respectable, but after heading round the back and seeing the large wooden shed leaning against the back of the main building through a crack in the fence, along with the smell that rushed out to meet me, I decided it was anything but. So after picking the lock on the gate and pressing a handkerchief over my nose and mouth to protect me from the raw stench of alcohol, I rapped the door a few times, calling out 'Health inspector; I've come to check your drains.' A few seconds of humourless laughter later, the door opened and I went inside.

After a couple of minutes of fairly robust back-and-forth with the eldest of the Barrett brothers, a pinch-faced Beagle who smelled nearly as bad as his hooch, he admitted that yes, he and his brother *had* had contact with Ms Bouchard – or a couple of her employees anyway – but no, they never had – and never would – be doing business with her. He then said that if I wanted to have this confirmed I could try having a word with his younger brother, Eric, once the surgeons at the hospital had wired his jaw back together. At which point the elder Barrett hobbled away with the aid of his cane and asked me if I'd like to contribute towards the cost of repairing his left knee, which Mimi's henchmutts had gone to work on after they'd socked Eric in the jaw. 'To say this stuff is pigswill I can live with,' the old Beagle said, waving his cane around. 'To say it's overpriced is plumb crazy.' When I failed to come up with an appropriate response, Barrett told me to close the gate on my way out, adding that if I *should* bump into Bouchard's lackey's I was to pass on his warmest regards.

Undeterred, I headed back round to the front of Belmont Avenue while I was in the vicinity and decided to give the soup kitchen at the far end of the street a try. The second I walked in a tall, thin English Setter with an unusually large black nose eyed me over by the vats of soup. Making my way towards him through tables crowded with various down-on-their-luck creatures tucking into bowls of thick grey broth, I knew, just knew, I was wasting my time.

'Bouchard, you say? I remember her – turned up with a photographer in tow. Didn't stay long after that, though.'

'Long enough to look down her nose at me and Hank,' said a passing Pug wearing what looked like a dirty boiler suit. 'Complained about the smell, half-filled our bowls and went. Stuck-up bitch.'

Thanking them for their time, I tried to keep my spirits up as I drove around looking for the second place on my list, Leary Way; but after nearly three quarters of an hour of driving round asking anyone who looked vaguely knowledgeable, they were lower than they had been when I'd left the soup kitchen. Finally deciding to ask someone who *would* be knowledgeable, I pulled in opposite a taxi and asked its driver if he could help me.

'Leary Way? Never heard of it,' the cabbie said. 'And if I ain't heard of it, it don't exist.'

'Are you sure?'

'Sure I'm sure,' he told me. 'Listen, I've been driving around this city since two days after The Terror. I know my streets.' So it looked like Vincent had misheard. Picking up a fare, the cabbie sped away.

While I'd been driving round getting nowhere it had started to rain. Winding up my window against this sudden cloudburst I drove off, pulled into the first quiet side street I found, switched off the engine and tried to decide what to do next. Only not very successfully, because the rain was bouncing off the car so hard I couldn't think straight, the drops running down the windshield the size of Elephant's tears. When the thunder started in with a noise like the grumblings from a giant's belly I gave up, deciding instead to take in the street around me.

Despite the conditions and the fact that it was pushing midnight, the street was pretty busy, full of the kind of furtive, solitary individuals you only ever seem to see in the dead of night. One of them was hobbling straight towards me – a creature of indeterminate gender covered from head to toe in a rain-darkened sou'wester. As it got closer I noticed how large its coat was, dwarfing the animal inside, its head buried deep within the hood. When it was a few feet away my scalp started to prickle; and when it was level with my side window, it stopped.

My view limited by the rain running down the glass, I watched as the figure bent slightly and two gloved paws emerged from within the pockets of the voluminous coat and clamped themselves roughly in the area where its knees should be, the wind and rain lashing at it mercilessly. Suddenly, the cowled head began to rock violently back and forth, momentarily creating in my mind the image of a ridiculously large Bird pecking at the ground. When the rumble of thunder gave way to a gigantic crack, the figure rocked even harder; finally, as a flare of bluish/white lightning flooded the street, the now illuminated creature hawked a ball of phlegm the size of a puppy's fist out of the hood and into the gutter. Then, apparently having done what it needed to do, it stuck its gloved paws back in its pockets and continued its trek up the street.

Not for the first time lately unnerved by something I didn't understand, I looked down and was surprised to see my gun in my paw. Putting it away, I rubbed at my face with my other paw as I waited for my pulse to subside. Finally calm, I got out my notebook and pencil and hoped that it'd be third time lucky with the leads Vincent had given me. Switching on the car's interior light, I looked down the list:

> Barrett Bros, Belmont Ave – Bootleg Hooch (soup kitchen?)
> Leary Way (?)
> Janklow's
> Quesnay's
> Bingham
> Osterlein
> Relf (Ralf?) Partnership

Scratching the first two leads off the list, I was about to draw a ring round the third when an odd little thought occurred to me. Turning back to the previous page in my notebook, I looked at the names Lance Shoebury had given me for the bar he'd mentioned. Then I looked back up the street for the hooded figure, but it was gone.

No matter. Smiling to myself, I added both names to the list, circled them and put the pencil and notebook back in my pocket. Vincent's leads weren't getting me anywhere, so why not? Maybe it's because I'm a Gumshoe and odd little connections like that tend to stick in my mind, but I decided to take what I'd just witnessed as a sign. Besides, I liked the bar's nickname, even if it didn't lead anywhere. So, switching off the inside light, I put the key in the ignition and headed over there. By the time I arrived it had even stopped raining.

Maybe it *was* a sign, after all.

23.

O'Riordan's Bar – also known to its patrons as the Coughing Fit Saloon thanks to the excessive strength and roughness of the liquor it sold, was as low-rent a place as its nickname suggested. Much later I found out that a large quantity of the rot-gut it sold came via the Barrett Brothers on Belmont Avenue. It was a small world right enough.

As I approached the bar, a greasy-furred Bearded Collie was downing the contents of a shot glass. 'Another,' he gasped, wiping the tears away from his eyes.

'I'll get this,' I told the barmutt, adding: 'Say, what do you guys do for fun around here?'

'You have what he's having,' he told me, slamming the hooch down in front of the Collie. 'Only in your case I'd give it a miss. *Definitely* too strong for pussy-cats.' At the other end of the bar, someone laughed. As it was true, I said nothing.

'Nice guy,' I said to the Bearded Collie as the barmutt walked away.

'He's just sore because he hasn't put the prices up this week.' He knocked back half of the glass. 'He's right though – if you guys can't drink, why the hell would you want to come to a dive like this?'

'A friend of mine said he might pop by,' I lied. 'Actually, you might have heard of him. Lance Shoebury.' Catching the bartender's eye, he made his way back over.

'Nope, name means nothing t'me,' the Collie said.

'Another for my friend here,' I said to the bartender.

'And what about you?' he scowled. 'You having anything this time?'

'Guess it'll have to be tuna oil for me,' I said. 'You charge for ice in a place like this?'

'No. I could spit in the glass too, if you like. I won't charge for that either.'

'Hold the spit,' I told him. 'Literally, if it makes you happy.' With another scowl he fixed our drinks.

Like in the soup kitchen earlier, sometimes you get a sense when something just isn't going to work, and after a half-hour of fairly discreet questioning I had nothing to show for it. As I was debating whether to buy the Collie another drink or not, he suddenly raised one of his paws and stuck it in my face.

'I thought you had a buddy showing up here,' he slurred. 'Where is he?' Ignoring the question I started to ask one of my own, but he cut me off. 'Hey, what's with the interrogation? Since you got here it's been question after question. You ain't a cop, are ya?'

Hearing the word 'cop' the barmutt looked over, as did an incredibly large Bulldog on the other side of the room; instinct told me that a nod from the barmutt and the Bulldog would throw me out of the joint faster than the Collie could throw back the contents of a shot glass.

'A cop? Hell no,' I said to the Collie. 'I was just making conversation, that's all. Being friendly.'

'Aw, ain't nobody been friendly to me since the day I was born,' the Collie whined. 'You know what? I think you *are* a cop! Well, I ain't talkin' to no flatfoot, mister. No sir.' And, as if to demonstrate how intent he was on not talking to me, he closed his eyes, slid off his barstool and fell backwards onto the sawdust.

The night not getting any younger, I took that as my cue to leave. Rising from my stool, I turned towards the door.

I'd only taken a few steps when there was an explosion of noise behind me. In the pool room beyond the bar there was a flurry of paws, and at its centre was the large Bulldog. A pool cue hurtled through the air towards the bar like a spear, crashing to the ground a few feet short, quickly followed by a small, greyish Terrier who landed a few feet behind it. He'd barely hit the floor when the Bulldog came stomping through from the pool room towards him. Picking the Terrier up by the scruff of the neck, he hurled the little guy towards the door, only falling short by a couple of feet. But instead of crawling out the door before the Bulldog had a chance to finish the job, the Terrier sprang back up and ran the length of the bar back towards the pool room, sidestepping the bigger Dog on the way. Skidding to a halt, he removed a shoe and sock and, grabbing pool-balls from the table, began stuffing them inside the sock. By the time the Bulldog got to him the sock was full; but before he had a chance to do anything about it the Terrier was swinging it at his head at some speed. Whacking the Bulldog on the temple with a loud, hollow *clonk,* the few conscious patrons in the bar cheered.

Smiling, I went into the pool room, where the Terrier was leaning against the table breathing hard, emptying the balls out of his sock.

'Where'd you learn a trick like that?' I asked, already knowing the answer.

'Yeah, sure I was there that night,' Dukey Fitzallan told me as he sat on the edge of the pool table fastening up his shoe, the unconscious Bulldog lying only a few feet away. 'I always used to get knocked about because of my size, but when I saw what that lady did, I thought *that's* how you protect yourself, know what I mean?'

'Sounds like you were rather taken with her,' I said.

'Nah. Too flashy for my taste – lots of jewellery – *and* she was wearing a fur coat on top of the one she was born with – not a fake fur either – a real one. Still, the guy she was with loved it.'

'Falconetti?'

'If you say so. He was a bit of a dummy. She was the smart one, anyone could see that.'

'I don't suppose you've seen her since?' I asked him and the barmutt, who'd also wandered over. 'I'm looking for her.' But neither had.

Taking out my notebook I went through my list, but besides what I realise now was a flicker of recognition when I mentioned the Barrett Brothers, I drew a blank. However, when I started tossing names at them they both reacted to Dash Norman, Dukey sneering, the barmutt sniggering.

'What?' I asked.

'Empty your pockets,' Dukey said.

'Excuse me?'

'Empty your pockets,' Dukey said again. 'Onto the table. Might be worth your while.'

Shrugging, I took out a few notes along with a pawful of loose change and put them on the table. Dividing the notes and coins into separate piles, Dukey scooped up the coins before handing me back the notes. Feeding a couple of the coins to the table and placing the rest on the edge, he racked up the balls, removed the triangle and split them apart, sinking two from the break-off.

'So it's not just pool balls in a sock you're good with,' I said.

'I'd play all night if I had the money,' Dukey said. 'That's what the argument with him was about.' He nodded at the Dog on the floor. 'Said I was hogging the table.' Poking his cue into the Bulldog's ribs, the Bulldog groaned a little.

'Okay,' Dukey said after taking a few more shots and sinking a few more balls, 'you want Dash Norman? Try Waldron's rooming house, room forty-six. Leave here and turn left. It's two blocks away. If he's not there, he has a storage unit in a building a couple minutes' further along the same road. Flat roof.'

'Thanks.' I went to put the notes beside the stack of change but Dukey shook his head.

'No need,' he said. 'The coins are enough.'

'It's rare I get information so cheaply.'

'Well, I try to be a good citizen,' Dukey informed me stiffly.

The bartender roared with laughter. 'The hell you do,' he said. 'Let me tell ya something, Shamus. In all the time I've been running this joint I've only ever seen Dukey lose twice at pool. You wanna take a guess who beat him both times?'

'One of those was a fluke,' Dukey snarled, miscuing his shot and nearly ripping the baize.

'Yeah, sure it was,' the bartender cooed. 'Anyways, how about you give me a hand to move this knucklehead out of the way? He's stinking up the place.' Bending down towards the Bulldog, the barmutt grabbed his feet. Sighing, Dukey leaned his cue against the table and grabbed his arms.

Leaving them to their burden I headed for the door, careful to avoid stepping on the Bearded Collie still sprawled out near the bar. 'Don't forget about this one,' I shouted to them.

'Oh, he'll be fine,' the barmutt assured me. 'He'll come to in about ten minutes or so. He usually does.'

24.

Ten minutes later I was standing in one of the cities' cleaner alleyways – one in which the garbage didn't quite reach the first floor windows – looking up at the rear of Waldron's rooming house, or more specifically the rusted metal staircase bolted to its wall, with a certain resignation.

The building, an ugly brown affair sitting a few feet back from the empty road, had a cockeyed sign in front of it propped up with bricks, announcing that rooms were still available. A few lights burned in windows, but none on the fourth floor. Trying various buzzers got me nowhere, neither did hammering on the front door. Slipping round the back, I spotted two possible entry points; open windows, one on the second floor and one on the fourth; but the only way up to them was via the aforementioned staircase. Pushing the image of large silhouetted beaks from my mind, I grabbed the wet metal handrail, shut out the smell of garbage as best I could and started to climb.

I had to take my time – besides being slippery with rain, each step I took produced groans and squeaks along with a slight wobble, making me wonder if the staircase was properly fastened to the wall. Eager to get inside as soon as possible however, I carried on regardless towards the second floor window.

A few feet away from it I held my breath and listened, but heard nothing. There were no curtains in the window, no knick-knacks on the windowsill and a gap almost wide enough for me to crawl through. Easing the window open a little wider, I grabbed the frame, put my foot on the sill and started to feel my way inside. But just as I was readying myself to jump down into the room my paw brushed against something, something thick and wet, and then I caught the unmistakeable smell of animal fur.

'Hey, what's the idea?' a panicked voice blurted out.

'Sorry,' I managed to splutter. 'Um, wrong room.'

'Don't worry about it,' the voice said. 'I done it myself before now. Good thing you woke me anyways. I coulda caught my death lying here. Damned window.' When they slammed it shut, I barely had time to get out of the way.

So it was back to the staircase. Taking a moment or two to let my pulse drop back into double digits, I set out once more. Thankfully there were other things to listen to this time other than the creaking stairs, like an argument about whose turn it was to wash the dishes and a blaring radio on the third floor. Finally reaching the open window on the fourth I listened intently, and as before heard nothing. Learning from my earlier mistake, I snapped on my flashlight and shone it into the darkened room, finding nothing, not even a stick of furniture. Taking a couple of deep breaths, I climbed inside.

Making my way through the tiny apartment, it looked like it hadn't been inhabited for quite a while. Standing before the front door I listened for noise in the corridor but there wasn't any. Even so, I let myself out in slow motion, and as I did looked at the number plate on the door: forty-four – Dash's was the next one along.

The door was so cheap picking the lock only took seconds. Easing it open, I dug the gun from my pocket, went inside.

Even from the hall the place felt empty, the air stale and heavy. Holding onto the gun anyway I took a look around, but besides a spare set of clothes in the closet and a pool cue next to the bed, there was nothing much to see. The storage unit it was then.

Able to leave in a slightly more civilised fashion than I'd arrived, I made my way down the stairs, the elevator apparently out of order. Walking down past the third floor corridor I heard yelling, the argument about dishes turning into something more serious. Even on the second floor landing I could still hear it. Directly above me I heard a door slam hard, soon followed by a low rumbling to my right; then there was an almighty clang and the building itself seemed to shake.

Racing over to the corridor window I looked out and down through the rising dust, not believing what I was seeing. Wanting to get a better look despite myself, I hurried down the stairs to the alley. Amazingly, by the time I arrived several animals were already there, the alley floodlit with light from back-room windows as those inside craned their necks looking at the ground.

Lying at an angle amongst the garbage like some huge metallic skeleton, the metal staircase rocked gently from side to side, the wall it had broken free from looking strangely naked to its left. But it was the staircase that really got my attention, the staircase I'd been walking on only minutes earlier, brought crashing to the ground by something as ordinary as the slamming of a door, its great *clang* echoing in my head, making my nerves sing.

It wasn't until something moved past me over to the left that I was able to look away; but I soon wished I hadn't. Projected against the naked wall by the lights inside the building, a silhouetted parade of oversized animals shuffled back and forth, hoping to get a better look at the damage; and the fact that none of them had feathers didn't provide any comfort. Trying not to think about it, I rubbed a paw roughly across my face and headed back to my car.

The flat-roofed building that was home to Dash Norman's storage unit was as suspiciously nondescript as places of that sort usually are, and at that hour of course shut up tight. Across the way, an all-night café's green neon light flickered on and off, giving substance to the puddles on the sidewalk. Inside the café, a scrawny feline stood behind the counter chewing gum, and with little else to do had decided to keep her eye on me. Trying to appear as inconspicuous as possible I looked down at my shoes, then up at the sky, before turning my attention to an imaginary speck of dust on my jacket. Two minutes later when I looked over at the café again she was still looking and still chewing. Finally deciding to risk whatever action she might take and to hell with it, I approached the building's entrance.

Something was banging close by; hopefully an open window. But getting closer I realised it wasn't a window at all, but the door rattling about in a badly-fitting frame. Well, it was worth a try… so I grabbed the door handle and pushed, but of course nothing happened. Looking back to the other side of the street, the waitress was still watching me, her arms now folded across her chest.

A tough crowd. Perhaps playing the forgetful card would help. Looking skyward again, I slapped my forehead, took my office keys from my pocket and held them up for her to see before turning away. Exchanging them for a little something I also had in my pocket I worked on the door, which luckily didn't take much longer to open than if I'd really had the keys. Ignoring the eyes I was sure were still on my back, I got out my gun and went inside.

Leaving the door slightly ajar, I had just enough light to see with. The place was full of small, bricked-off rooms left and right, the air smelling of cold damp stone, an ancient and somehow lonely smell. Inching forwards, I saw that every unit had its metal doors raised, each unit waiting to be occupied; all except one, which was closed. Only its door wasn't quite flush with the ground.

Dropping to my knees, I flicked on my flashlight, played it through the gap; and as I did I noticed the smell, a smell that even the cold, damp walls couldn't mask, and saw a sight that made me wish that Cats *could* drink: Dash Norman, sprawled across the stone floor in a pool of blood, a hole in his chest so big you could put your fist in it. Because of the thickness of the walls, it was hard to imagine anyone nearby hearing anything. Getting up off my knees I dusted myself down and went over to the café.

'Handy, you finding your keys like that all of a sudden,' the scrawny waitress said as she chewed. 'You know, I oughta call the police.'

'I'll save you the trouble if you can change this,' I said, handing her a bill from my pocket. 'What's the coffee like here?'

'Awful.'

'Just how I like it.'

Feeding some of the change she gave me into the telephone, I called the police station and asked for Dingus. While I was on hold the waitress came over with the coffee. Her name badge said she was called Lulu. I was just about to take a sip when a voice in my ear said, 'Hello?'

'Dingus? It's me.' Giving him the details, he said he'd be right over. Hanging up, I took a sip of the coffee, winced, and sat down to wait.

'Is it always like this in here?' I asked Lulu, spooning sugar into my coffee.

'He tastes the coffee and then asks,' she muttered. 'Incidentally, you can add as much sugar as you like. It won't help none.'

'Maybe not,' I said. 'But I've got a sweet tooth. And besides –'

I was just spooning in my fifth sugar when I saw a car – the first one I'd seen since I'd been in the area – out of the corner of my eye. My first thought was that it must be a police car, but it was the wrong colour and didn't stop. And its driver was feline and female, a black Chartreaux with a heart-shaped face.

Spilling coffee everywhere, I tore out of the café and jumped into my car round the corner. She wasn't exactly cruising, but with the roads empty I was able to keep her in sight pretty easily on the long straight road. A mile or so later when she slowed down and took a left into the parking lot of an all-night restaurant, I decided to take my chance. Gunning the accelerator, I roared into the parking lot as Mimi was parking her car. Slamming on the brakes I pulled up a few feet behind her, the engine still running. Before she had a chance to turn I was out of the car, a paw on her shoulder.

'Rule number one, sweetcheeks – never return to the scene of a crime,' I said, spinning her round. 'In fact my advice would be don't go near it at all, because –'

In hindsight, the slap across the face I received for my overfamiliarity was fair punishment for letting my mouth do the work when my eyes would've done a better job; because whatever superficial similarities *this* Chartreaux had with Mimi Bouchard, it plainly wasn't her. As I gawked at her, shocked at my mistake, she scoured her vocabulary for suitable words to chastise me with. When she couldn't find them, she kicked me hard on the shin.

'And *don't* call me sweetcheeks,' she said, stomping away.

By the time I'd quit rubbing my face and shin I didn't much fancy returning to the storage unit and explaining my wild goose-chase to the Lieutenant. So, trusting in his ability to manage without me, I kept going along the road I'd been travelling, which would eventually get me back to the city. Thinking about Vincent's remaining leads and where – if anywhere – they might take me, it occurred to me as I drove along that I wasn't a million miles away from where a certain Rabbit spent his evenings. If anybody could help me with them it would be him, so making a slight adjustment to my journey, I made a beeline for Harvey.

Or rather, Laurence.

25.

The Adelphi, the city's premiere casino, was situated in its own grounds about five minutes away from the centre of the city, surrounded by thick trees and enough grass to keep a herd of cattle happy for a year. Parking up amongst the large, shiny black cars in the circular courtyard, I made my way through the knots of chauffeurs in immaculate suits standing around smoking cigarettes and chewing the fat. Close by, in the centre of the courtyard, a large fake marble fountain sprayed water high into the night sky.

Like guns, I didn't much care for gambling dens. In a strange way they remind me of churches; I don't really understand what goes on inside them, but the architecture's usually interesting and they're quite nice to poke around in before the fun and games start. Crunching along the gravel path and nodding to the obligatory Ape on the door, I went into the bar.

I always got the feeling that most of the Adelphi's patrons didn't go there with the intention of gambling, only to drink and relax. But most of them ended up in the casino eventually; nature usually demanded it. And once there the odds were stacked against them.

The bar, a semi-circular affair on the left in a

tastefully decorated room, was a living picture of mirrored glass, smooth shiny surfaces and smiling bar staff. On the opposite side of the room the all-Cat house band, dressed in identical off-white tuxedos, strummed, brushed and plucked assorted instruments on a raised dais whilst trying not to look too bored. With the exception of a small area in front of the stage for dancing, the rest of the space was taken up with bulky, chocolate-coloured couches at the ends of which were large metal free-standing ashtrays filled with sand. The mood was convivial, the drinks were strong but reasonably priced and there was an endless supply of free bar snacks, usually nuts and anchovies, the latter for the few felines in attendance.

So far, so good – for the Adelphi if no-one else. Because for some inexplicable reason the air conditioning never seemed to work; which, along with the consumption of all those salty nibbles meant that more drinks were bought, in turn leading to more visits to the washrooms: both of which happened to be situated on the far side of the casino. And once there, filled with the bravado provided by the double-strength hooch, it was amazing the number of animals who couldn't resist all that glamour and excitement…

Looking around I didn't see anyone I recognised, least of all any overgrown bunnies, so pushing my way through the room, I parted the beaded curtain at the far end and stepped over the threshold into the casino.

As usual, the place was a sea of tuxedos in a permanent fog of sweat, perfume, cologne and cigar smoke, not helped by the slightly dimmed lighting. There was however some colour among the gloom, like the pair of yellow Parrots by the crap table wearing matching powder-blue dickie bows held in place by long elastic, and the squat Hamster with the monocle over by the slot machines in his green zoot suit. But I wasn't interested in them; I was interested in the large white Rabbit with slightly protruding teeth at the roulette table, an unusually small stack of plastic chips in front of him. Catching his eye for the briefest of moments, he blinked and looked away. Walking past his table, I made for the washrooms.

Digging the smallest coin I could find out of my pocket, I handed it to the snooty little Shih-Tzu standing outside. With a disapproving little movement of the head he let me pass, into a world of gold-plated taps, gleaming white tiles and hushed calm. Turning the taps on full, I made a pretence of washing my paws as I waited for Harvey – or, as the city's more financially solvent members knew him, Laurence – to arrive.

The idea of meeting Harvey – or indeed Laurence – in a place like this a year ago would have been ridiculous; not least because Laurence didn't exist then. A year ago, it was just Harvey. But after having his teeth sawn off by his neighbour the summer before last, Harvey had gradually changed; and the transformation wasn't just a physical one. After a couple of years of being effectively imprisoned by the two white bars constantly growing in his face, Harvey realised he'd missed out on a lot of living; and while selling donuts on 67th Street provided a bit of regular income it didn't exactly serve up the thrills he was looking for. So one night, not long after coming back to my office for his old job, he decided to dip into the money he'd saved from the donut stall, hire himself a tuxedo, and minus teeth have a night out at the casino; and as it turned out, Harvey and casinos were a very good fit. Like informing, they provided an element of risk; but unlike informing, from that very first visit right up to the present day, they'd also by and large provided him with sizeable amounts of cash. He'd had his dips, but ever since leaving the Adelphi that first night with his pockets stuffed full of bills, he'd made so much money that he was able to afford the rent on a pad in the centre of town. Only this pad wasn't for Harvey – it was for Laurence, the persona that Harvey had been cultivating as his stock rose in the city's gambling establishments. Taking his cue – and name – from a character in a radio serial he was fond of, Laurence enjoyed the best of what life had to offer; whilst Harvey, complete with his oversized gnashers, continued to live out in the sticks. And besides me, Taki, the Mouse and a few others, nobody knew the truth.

Because I still did most of my business with the downtrodden and scruffy Harvey, the sight of Laurence always gave me a shock. Looking years younger minus his teeth, and resplendent as usual in his white suit, shining spats, salmon-pink tie and matching breast pocket handkerchief, Harvey/Laurence looked about as at home as it was possible to look in a casino.

'How goes it, Benjamin? Or shouldn't I ask?' he said after exchanging pleasantries with the Shih-Tzu, the rich, oaky, cultured voice he used on such occasions never failing to surprise or amuse me.

Before I could respond, he walked me over to the rear of the washroom and turned on the nearest of the gold taps. 'How's things, Mr S?' he asked, his accent slipping somewhere between Laurence's and Harvey's.

'Oh, ticking along,' I replied, handing him my notebook. 'Any of these names mean anything to you?'

Squinting at my scrawl, he scanned the list. 'Ah, you know about the Barrett Brothers then... Leary Way – no. Janklow's – only that there's a jewellers of that name on Turnbull Street. Quesnay's – never heard of it. Ditto Bingham. Os – well, I'll be a Monkey's uncle,' turning to me he grinned, his clean white teeth sparkling in the bright light of the washroom.

'What?' I asked.

'You're a lucky Cat, is what. So lucky in fact I'm going to ask you for a number between one and thirty-eight.' Folding his arms, the grin got wider.

Confused, I blurted out the first number I could think of. 'Okay, twenty-six. How does that help?'

'There's a chance it might not,' he replied. 'But when someone comes in here looking for a guy in the dark like that and he's in the next room, I figure that someone must be on some kind of a lucky streak, which is more than I am right now. And I get the impression the same is true for Mr Osterlein.'

Slowly, my brain caught up with his words. 'Osterlein's *here*?'

'He certainly is.'

'Show me.'

'All in good time, dear boy,' he said, patting me on the shoulder. 'First, I have to use the facilities.' Striding over to one of the stalls, he began to whistle something that sounded like it belonged in a concert hall and definitely not on 67th Street. The melody taking root in my brain, I shuffled past the Shih-Tzu and back into the casino.

No doubt about it; Laurence and Harvey were different creatures all right.

'He's the one at the blackjack table,' he whispered into my ear, 'next to the Bengal with the pearl necklace.'

As Laurence took up his place by the roulette wheel I took a good look at Osterlein. He was an ageing Pewter Longhair with grey fur and long, white whiskers. Twitching imperceptibly beside a small pile of chips, the black cigarillo in his left paw sent a fine streamer of smoke up towards his small, serious mouth.

'What do you know about him?' I asked.

'Beside the fact he's a lousy card player? Only his name. And I only know that because I heard a croupier using it as they were trying to calm him down one night. Always seems to have cash to burn though. Well, when he comes in, at any rate.'

'Looks like you have that in common this evening,' I said, nodding at Laurence's small pile of chips. 'Maybe your winning streak's coming to an end.'

Laurence chuckled. 'Such negativity in one so young. You've been pounding those streets too long, my friend. Besides, you're forgetting – now I have your lucky number. Speaking of which, I think it's high time we put it to the test.' Turning his attention to the table, Laurence bet everything he had on twenty-six.

Not wanting to see a fool and his money parted, I looked over to Osterlein only to find that he'd pulled the same stunt, the cigarillo now in his mouth, jiggling up and down. From the roulette table I heard the whirring of the wheel and the clacking of the ball as it spun round it, the wheel slowing, Osterlein's loss holding more interest than Laurence's. But as I watched him fidget waiting for the turn of the cards, I could still hear the ball as it continued to bounce around the roulette wheel a few feet away, louder and louder, the gap between bounces getting shorter and shorter, reduced finally to a succession of rapid little clicks, followed by a brief moment of silence and the croupier calling out:

'Twenty-six – black.'

Stunned, I looked away from Osterlein and down at the roulette table and the huge pile of chips Laurence was drawing towards him. By the time I got my attention back to Osterlein his game was over. Angrily stubbing the remains of his cigarillo into a nearby sand bucket, he stomped away from the table in disgust.

'Well, I guess I'll be seeing you around, Larry,' I said, slapping the Rabbit on the shoulder. 'And thanks.'

'Ha! Thank *you*,' he called out to me, laughing as he placed another bet. 'And remember, Benjamin – you're on a roll. Milk it for all it's worth.'

I was about level with the blackjack table where Osterlein had stood when he said that, and it brought me to a stop. Because ever since the incident in the side street which led me to the Coughing Fit Saloon, and despite the odd moments of unease I felt and all the rest of it – not least of which was the fact both my clients were in police custody – I had the feeling that finally, *finally* things were turning in my favour. And it felt good. *Really* good.

Remember, Benjamin – you're on a roll. Milk it for all it's worth.

Squeezing my way through the throng of sweating animals, I headed after Osterlein.

Out in the parking lot, the air was cool and sweet after the intense heat and odours of the casino. Not that I had much time to breathe it in, as Osterlein was already in his car and revving his engine. Scurrying over to my own, I gave him a few seconds to get going and set off after him.

Taking a right out of the grounds, he chugged up a steep hill, slid down the other side and took a couple of right turns towards the kind of apartment block a broke Pewter Longhair might go and smoke cigarillos in. Narrowing the gap between us, I was wondering how to play the next bit – either intercept him in the parking lot or let him get inside first – when a car shot out of the lot past Osterlein and then past me, my headlights illuminating its interior and passengers for the briefest of seconds: a prematurely balding Mastiff with slightly bulging eyes in the driver's seat, and, sitting beside him, a black Chartreaux with luminescent orangey-brown eyes.

For the second time that night I found myself looking at the face of Mimi Bouchard – only this time it definitely *was* her.

Laurence, it seemed, was right.

I *was* on a roll.

26.

Yanking the steering wheel to the left as hard as I could, I just about managed to avoid hitting a fire hydrant on the other side of the street before getting the car back under control, all the while watching their tail-lights receding in the distance. Stomping down on the gas, I made up some ground but not much. Then, instead of heading back to town as I'd expected, they veered right down a poorly-lit road leading god-knows-where and slowed right down, the gap between us diminishing. Either they somehow hadn't realised they were being followed or were looking for somewhere suitable to waylay me. I was pretty sure it was the latter. Seconds later I was proved right when their car slowed further, disappearing behind a ratty-looking dump of a building beside a fenced-in vacant lot strewn with garbage sacks.

As I had moments earlier with Osterlein, I wondered how I should play this; the difference this time was that I was outnumbered. So pulling up in the stinking alley just before the building and getting out of the car, it was with a heavy heart that I started to go for my gun, only for a voice from the shadows to call out:

'Paws where I can see them, if you please.'

Raising them I smiled. 'My apologies. Thinking I'm about to get plugged always makes me nervous.' Casting my eyes around quickly I looked for Hagen, saw nothing but shadows. 'I have to say, this place isn't up to your usual standards.'

'Oh Mr Spriteman,' Mimi said wearily, remaining out of sight. 'I had hoped our paths wouldn't cross again, but now that they have perhaps we can resolve matters amicably without anybody getting "plugged" – I hate all that unpleasantness. I seem to remember the first time we met wrongly thinking you were looking for money. If, however, this time –'

'Save your breath,' I interrupted. 'But if you have money to burn you could toss a little of it Osterlein's way – he seems to be on a losing streak at the casino. Unless you just posted some through his mailbox while he was out.'

In the seconds that followed the air seemed to become thin with supressed anger. 'If you don't want money, what do you want?' she snapped.

'The same thing I wanted that first time we met,' I told her. 'To find out who killed Gino Chomsky. Nothing more, nothing less.'

She laughed but it had steel in it. 'All this aggravation over a yapping mutt; my god,' she said almost to herself. 'Is it really worth it for the pittance you might not even get from that ridiculous little Chihuahua?' she pronounced it *she-wow-wow*. 'Such a waste of your precious time, don't you think? I, on the other hand *can* pay you – handsomely. And all you'd have to do is walk away.'

It was my turn to laugh. 'You'll no more let me walk away from here than anyone else who gets in your way,' I told her. 'Including those closest to you. Incidentally, the body in the barrel up at what's left of your house? A nice touch, to be sure. Say what you like about him, but Falconetti certainly taught you well, *Betty.*'

She didn't reply; at least not verbally. From the shadows I heard an ugly scraping sound, claws raking brickwork.

'I had hoped we could talk sensibly Mr Spriteman,' she said eventually, emerging from the gloom, a slight black Cat wearing another animal's fur on top of her own. 'But I'm obviously wasting my time. Aidy –' She smiled suggestively past me as she walked away, and as she did I cursed myself for being a chump, realising that while we'd been talking, Hagen, under cover of darkness, his scent masked by the stink of garbage, had been sneaking up behind me.

I was in the process of turning round when he pounced. 'Mimi don't like being called that,' he snarled, grabbing the front of my shirt along with a couple of fistfuls of fur, 'and I don't like to hear it. I mean I *really* don't like to hear it.'

Despite my predicament I found the mixture of anger and hurt in his eyes made me smile. 'You don't honestly think she's interested in an Ape like you?' I said, my voice a strangulated half-laugh as I was lifted off the ground. 'She's taking you for a sucker, Aidy old man.'

'We're crazy about each other,' he growled. 'When all this is over we're going someplace warm to start a new life.'

'Then you'll need to buy a hat,' I said, barely able to get the words out. 'Because it looks to me like you're prone to sunburn.' Gritting my teeth, I raised my paws and raked my claws across his bald spot. Howling, he dropped me to the floor where I lay amongst the garbage gasping like a landed fish.

'You know, I'm real glad how this has turned out,' he said standing above me, blood dripping down his forehead. 'Since all this blew up Mimi and me have been calling in favours, collecting money, and it's been real disappointing because everyone's paid up and I haven't got to teach anyone a lesson. But Mimi, she said Osterlein would probably need to be taught a lesson 'cos he wouldn't have anything to give us. Only he wasn't there. Then he was. But so were you, so I didn't get the chance. But you know what? I think you probably deserve it more than he does.'

Yanking me up off the ground with what remained of my chest fur and shirt, he hurled me several feet through the air towards the chain-link fence bordering the lot. Unfortunately I hit one of the metal posts spine first, the metal chiming as clear as a bell, my fall partially broken by overflowing trash bags; but I'd barely landed amongst them when Hagen was reaching down towards me again.

Aiming a blow at him was impossible as was drawing the gun, so I had to think quickly. My claws still out, I used them to slit open a couple of the garbage bags, scrabbling around in the rubbish frantically for anything that might help delay the pummelling I was about to get. Almost straight away my paws closed around two objects; the one in my left paw was soft and cold and not exactly solid; but the thing in my right, despite being slimy, did at least have sharp edges.

This time with very little fur left to grab Hagen picked me up in a bear-hug, squeezing the air from my chest as he lifted, his grip so tight I almost dropped the garbage I was holding; yelling with pain and effort, I managed to get both my paws up towards his face and see what I was about to defend myself with: a rotten chunk of watermelon and the boned carcass of a fish.

Leading with my left, I squashed the watermelon into his ugly mug, causing him to loosen his grip; then I hit him with my right, doing my best to jam the skinned fish down his gullet. Half blinded by the cantaloupe and half choking on the carcass, he finally raised both paws to his face, leaving me to fall to the floor; and, taking my chance while he stood wiping the gunk from his face and removing the bone from his throat, I raised my boot and aimed a blow where nobody likes to be kicked. It wasn't as hard as I would've liked, but it was enough to double him over.

'Okay, Aidy, you've had your fun now,' Mimi called out sweetly from around a corner. 'We really need to go.'

'You're a fool Hagen,' I said as we both tried to get our breaths. 'You've killed Wareham for her and I'm willing to bet Dash Norman too. How many more? You think you and her are going off to play happy families? She's playing you the same way she played Falconetti. And look what happened to him.'

'Wareham got what was coming to him,' Hagen snarled. 'And Dash was a liability, the amount of stuff he smoked. As for Falconetti –'

'Oh, Aidy...' the voice, a touch impatient, was closer now.

'As for Falconetti, he didn't know how to handle her. So long, flatfoot.'

Charging at me before I had a chance to react, his blood and garbage smeared face was soon blotted out by the boot coming towards me.

And that, for a while, was that.

27.

I can't have been out too long because when I awoke I could still feel the imprint of Hagen's boot through the fur on my chin, which was now the size of an apple. Needless to say, it and my head ached. Wondering why he hadn't killed me, I wiped off as much of the garbage as I could, before tentatively getting to my feet and limping to my car, slumping heavily in the driver's seat. After giving myself a few minutes to think about how good it would feel to go home, take a long bath, clean up my wounds and have a better sleep than the one I'd just had in the garbage, I got back on the road and retraced the path I'd taken earlier which had led me to Osterlein's apartment building. If Mimi and Hagen were just about to split, I might not have long to find them, and with no better – or other – leads open to me, Osterlein was my best bet. The fact that he owed Mimi money in itself didn't seem that important, but knowing why she'd handed it over in the first place could be and might get me closer to her, me being on a roll and all. If I wanted to wrap up the case, it had to.

Casting my eye over the little name plates on the wall outside told me Osterlein was in apartment 88. Pressing half a dozen buzzers at random, I hit the jackpot despite the late hour.

'You ain't getting any quicker, Eric,' an unamused voice barked out at me from the fourth floor.

'Uh-huh,' I mumbled, listened. Evidently whoever was on the fourth floor listened back. Then just as I thought I was going to have to mumble something else, the door unlocked and I went inside.

Although I doubted Mimi would've returned while I was out cold, I took no chances. Taking the elevator to the seventh floor I crept along a corridor, found a door leading up to the eighth and tiptoed along until I found apartment 88. Listening outside, all was quiet. Not needing the little gizmo which had got me into Dash Norman's storage unit earlier, I counted to three and burst inside.

I found him damn near curled up in a ball on a couch, scared stiff. He was in such a state I don't think he even noticed I was covered in trash.

'Who're y –'

'Tell me what you know about Mimi Bouchard,' I interrupted.

The mere mention of her made him flinch. 'I –'

'I need to know where she is. I know she was here – she shot out of your parking lot as you were coming home. I'm sure you saw her. I was right behind you.' I spoke quickly but kindly, trying to make him understand. Then I saw the scotch bottle by his side.

'You've been drinking that?' I said, pointing at it. 'You know we can't. We can't –'

'She's going to *kill* me,' he whined.

'No,' I told him. 'She's leaving town, she won't be back. She's –'

'You're not *listening!* She's going to *kill* me.' Reaching forward with a trembling paw, he picked up a piece of paper from the table in front of him and passed it over.

He had the lights down so low I had to squint to make it out. But written in small print in neat, rounded letters the following message was plain enough:

Next time it will be your throat. X

Above it an arrow pointed towards the top of the page. Looking over at Osterlein, his eye flickered momentarily across the room before turning away. Following his gaze, the only thing I could see in the murk was a large oblong in the corner of the room, probably a tallboy. Stepping over to the nearest light I flicked it on, bringing the tallboy into relief – and the long, thin gash running down the side of it.

'She – has this dagger,' Osterlein told me, his voice as small as a kitten's. 'She showed it to me the last time she was here looking for the money I owed. The handle was covered in jewels. It was pretty. She said it was a gift from her boyfriend. Then she smiled and said she'd killed him with it.' He looked up at me, sniffed.

'A dagger...'

He started to say something else but I didn't hear it; I was too busy looking at that long, thin gash on the tallboy, my mind swirling with sounds and images: the ripping noises I heard when I antagonised Mimi in her home, the slash-mark in the cushion; that ugly scraping sound I'd heard earlier on the brickwork; Plummer in the alley, saying Moseley's throat had been cut; every one of them caused by the rending of claws – or so I'd thought. Seeing the truth, my mind raced even faster, filling in the gaps, working out the details, piecing everything together until I could picture it all in my head, as clear as sunshine for the briefest of moments; then realising it would have to wait when I remembered the reason I'd come here in the first place: to see if I could get a lead on where Mimi was heading; only I couldn't get a word in edgewise because Osterlein had decided he wanted to confess.

'Wanna know how we met? A City Planning Department Committee. Not the Adelphi or a swanky bar – a City Planning Department Committee. You ever been to one of those things? They're as boring as hell. So what was someone like *that* doing there? First break we had, I was determined to ask her. But I never got the chance because *she* came over to talk to *me!* And you know what? For the first time in my life I was the most important animal in the world – not just some drudge in the Planning Department. I didn't know then she was on other committees, pulling the same stunt! Next thing I knew I was telling her my life story, the gambling debts I'd picked up –'

'Listen Osterlein,' I butted in, 'under different circumstances I'd love to hear this, believe me, but –'

'–*then* she makes a suggestion. Oh, I can see what she was doing *now*, but at the time –' Glugging back another finger or two of scotch he carried on.

'She said there was this freeway at the back of her property – one of those that wasn't in use because it was full of trash. She'd heard a rumour that the city was planning to clean them up and get them reopened. Or'narily she said she'd be in favour of such a scheme, but if that *partic'lar* freeway was reopened, the noise would be det – detre – bad for her business.'

'So let me guess – she said if you could arrange it so such a clean-up didn't take place behind her Salon she'd pay off your gambling debts.'

'And then some. At that point I didn't know the *real* reason she wanted the freeway left as it was. You know about what goes on upstairs in the Salon, right? Course you do. Anyway, when the list of freeways to be cleaned up was drafted the one running past the back of her place wasn't on it. And *that* shoulda been the end of it,' he said, taking another slug from the bottle. 'But oh no, I couldn't leave it at that. The money she gave me? Blew the whole lot – boom. So I went back to her for more, and she gave me it. Maybe she thought I'd be able to get her more information, I don't know. Only when I didn't pay her back quick enough she started coming round, and there was the incident with the knife –' He scrabbled around for the bottle on the floor, missed, carried on. 'You any idea what it's like, spending all your time in casinos, stealing from the place you work for just to get the stake? It ain't no pic –'

By now I'd heard more than enough and was just about to tell him so, yell that all I wanted to hear was if he knew where Mimi was headed. But something about the expression on his face stopped me, and it took me a few seconds to work out what it was: it was the look, the *realisation,* that no matter what he tried to do now, and no matter how hard he tried to do it, it was already too late.

Perhaps seeing the same realisation on my face he stopped talking. A split second later he began ejecting the whisky he'd drunk even more quickly that he'd put it away.

'It's not even mine,' he said when he'd finished, wiping his fur and coughing. 'A Retriever I know brought it round to drink when he came to play poker. I thought it might help.'

I shook my head. 'Come on,' I said, leading him away from the mess. 'I'll help you get cleaned up.'

Figuring I'd earned the privilege, I made two calls on Osterlein's phone while he was in the shower – one to the Morgue to see if Clancy was back – apparently he was, but was none too happy about it – and one to the station, leaving a message for Dingus to meet me at the Morgue.

'You know, when I saw her coming out of the lot towards me like that,' Osterlein said with a shudder as he came out of the bathroom, 'I really thought that was it. You're certain she's leaving town?'

'That's what Hagen said before he started to beat the crap out of me,' I told him. 'If she'd meant to kill you she'd have come back here right away.'

'I don't suppose it makes any difference anyhow. Did I hear you speaking to the police just now?'

'Yeah. Why?'

'Could you drop me off there? I don't fancy driving after –' he pointed to the near-empty bottle, now on the table.

'Well, I wasn't going that way, but sure. One question first: do you have *any* idea where she might be heading?' Thinking for a second, he shook his head.

'I didn't think so. Okay, let's go.'

The first few minutes we were in the car he was quite chatty. 'Thanks for helping me tidy myself up back there,' he said, rooting around in his pockets for a cigarillo and a lighter. 'You didn't have to do that.'

'Don't mention it. It's not as if I wasn't filthy to begin with.' Looking over at me, he finally noticed how dishevelled I was. 'So – the cops. What are you going to tell them?'

'Everything – everything that's been eating me up these past weeks,' he said, blowing a cloud of smoke up to the car's ceiling. 'I can't live with it any longer. If they throw the book at me, so be it.' Tilting his head back and breathing through his nostrils, two streamers of smoke vanished into the cloud. 'Yep. So be it.'

From that point on he didn't speak – just sat and smoked and stared out the window. Even when we entered the station he kept quiet. Telling him to take a seat, I went over to speak to the Desk Sergeant who'd been on duty earlier.

'That's the third one you've brought in tonight that looks like that,' he said, looking over at Osterlein. 'What happened to him anyways?'

Turning, I found Osterlein sitting perfectly still in a corner staring off into space, lips silently working.

'Same thing as happened to the other two,' I told the Desk Sergeant. 'Mimi Bouchard got to him.'

Knowing we had that in common, I headed for the Morgue.

28.

Stepping out of the elevator, I found Dingus sitting on a plastic seat at the far end of the corridor. I was still some distance away when he looked towards me, wrinkling his nose. 'What's that smell?' he said.

'There you go, bringing my smell into it again. It's fish heads, if you must know. I've taken to shampooing my fur with them. It'll be all the rage one day.'

As I spoke a furious metallic clattering boomed out from behind the doors ahead.

'It's been like this since I got here,' Dingus told me. 'He wasn't much better when I saw him at the Dash Norman shooting. Speaking of which – where were you? What have you found out? And why are we here?'

Glossing over my encounter with the Mimi-that-wasn't and telling him what happened with the real one and Hagen, Dingus listened intently. 'After that I went back to Osterlein's and this time I got to speak to him. He's into Mimi for some serious money, so it's fortunate he wasn't in when she called round. But she did leave him a little warning with a dagger she had – a dagger she told him was a gift from Falconetti and which she'd later used to kill him. After our chat with Vincent I'd half assumed that Mimi had shot him and stuck him in the barrel.'

'But we both saw that body together,' Dingus said. 'There was no knife-wound on it.'

'We weren't looking for one. And even if we had been I doubt we'd have seen it by flashlight in that murky basement. The point is, she has a dagger and she knows how to use it. And, as I learned from Hagen, she's currently calling in debts and favours and settling a few scores before she skips town. On top of that, she's the kind of animal prone to insane bursts of rage.'

'So?'

'So I don't think Sascha and Sadie killed Moseley. I think Mimi did.'

'But –'

'Think about it. If she's angry at anyone at the moment, it's the Chomsky's – if they hadn't called me in, none of this would be happening. So she wants them sorted out. But she has to be careful about it – she can't risk going round the front of the street in case the cops are watching the Salon, but she might be able to get into Montcrieff Terrace from the back via the abandoned freeway if there's no-one lurking around. And as luck would have it, Freeman had to leave early that night. So the coast was clear.

'She sends Moseley on ahead – either to do the deed himself or to soften up the Chomsky's before Mimi finishes them off. When he doesn't come back, she goes to see what the problem is. She gets to the alley behind the Pawnbrokers and sees the shape Moseley's in after his encounter with Sascha and Sadie and she's boiling over with fury – at him, the Chomsky's – everyone. She has an idea. She grabs the weakened Moseley round his neck and gives him the closest shave he's ever had in his life, and leaves. And when the body is found suspicion will immediately fall on the Chomsky's.'

'But Benji, Sascha and Sadie already admitted to

Moseley's murder. And their account matches what Plummer said in the alley – Moseley was walloped in the stomach and his throat was cut.'

'And I don't doubt that's what happened. What I doubt it whether Sascha was actually strong enough to kill him. We know she has a temper, and I think she took a swing at him and caught him in the throat – but hard enough to produce all that blood with her claws alone? The body was soaked in it.'

'We didn't see the wound,' Dingus put in.

'No – and in the dark neither would Sascha. And I'm guessing in her panicked state there probably seemed a lot more blood than there was. And the following morning when she found Moseley in the alley she'd have seen nothing *but* blood – so much it covered up the wound inflicted by Mimi, reinforcing her belief that she did it. And when she confessed –'

'We assumed she must have done it,' Dingus finished.

'Right. Maybe if Clancy had been there it would've been different. *He'd* have taken a good look at the corpse instead of a quick glance like Plummer did and told us what really caused the wound.' Behind the Morgue doors, the metallic clatter continued. 'Perhaps it's worth mentioning that to him,' I suggested. 'But we need to know one way or the other.'

A crash noisier than anything that had gone before made us both jump. 'You don't want to ask him yourself?' Dingus said.

'It'll sound better coming from you,' I said, patting him on the shoulder.

Throwing up his paws in surrender, Dingus opened the door.

Somehow despite all the noise he was making, Clancy heard us and turned to face us, a brain pan in his paw.

'Oh great. Just what I needed,' he shouted. 'My boat's at the bottom of the marina, I've spent so long in the water I've damned near got webbed feet, I'm up to my neck in corpses and now *you* show up! What do you want?'

'I need you to check a couple of bodies for me, one in particular. You see, we were at a crime scene earlier with this guy Plummer, and –'

For a second I thought Clancy's eyes were going to fall out. *'Plummer?'* he exploded. 'They've been using *him* in my place? Not that he's done anything in here – he probably brought the bodies in and went to the nearest bar!'

'That's what I smelled in the alley,' Dingus said, slapping his forehead. 'Bourbon – but the aftershave he was wearing was so strong it masked it.'

'Knowing him he probably drank that too,' Clancy spat. 'When I see Ashton –' stopping himself just as he was about to blow a gasket, he took a deep breath. 'Okay. What was it you said you wanted?'

'The causes of death for two animals. It shouldn't take more than a few seconds.'

'Names?'

'Falconetti and Moseley.'

'Right.' Stomping around the room, he pulled out two metal drawers. 'Any preference which one I look at first?'

'Falconetti.'

'Fine,' he said, picking up the notes. '"Found in a barrel in the ruins of a burning building". Interesting.'

Turning his attention to the desiccated body, he went over it slowly.

Carefully raising the head, a long gash resembling a slash-mark on an old tire was revealed across the throat of the mummified corpse.

While Dingus and I exchanged glances Clancy began examining Moseley, this time starting at the throat. 'Same as the other one. Throat's been cut – and deeply,' he informed us, his voice muffled as he rooted around. 'This is the one you saw Plummer at, right? I recognise the awful writing on the notes.'

'That's right. He took a quick look and said the throat was cut.'

'Well, he got that right. But knowing Plummer he probably thought it was done by *this*.' Straightening up, Clancy held up what looked like a Cat's claw just long enough to remind me of the one missing from Sascha's paw before dropping it in a metal dish beside the body.

Rubbing a paw across his face, Dingus said, 'But the main wound – it's the same as the one on Falconetti? The same weapon, perhaps?'

'I won't know for sure until later, but I'd say it's probable. Both wounds in the same region, too.'

'And the claw?'

'Further down. Punctured the skin but that was all. You didn't seriously think –'

'No, no – of course not. Thanks, Clance.'

'Thank *you*. Now I can get back to cleaning up this pigsty –' Slamming the metal drawers shut, we left him to it.

'I can't believe I missed the bourbon,' Dingus said as we headed for the elevator. 'And I should've asked Plummer for more details about Moseley, or taken a look myself.'

'You had an off day, that's all. Maybe all that smoke up at Mimi's earlier affected you,' I said. 'It certainly got to the Mouse.'

'Well, if it got to you it's had the opposite effect,' Dingus said, lighting up his drug of choice in the confines of the elevator. 'The way you figured all that out was something else.'

'Well, I figured it out eventually. I don't think it had anything to do with the dope though.'

'No?'

'Nah. Just hitting my stride, that's all.'

I began to say something else, but decided against it. Not for the first time though, Dingus seemed to read my mind.

'Forgive me for saying so Benji, but you don't seem as pleased by the outcome as you might be.'

Murmuring something non-committal, I looked away. 'Like I said, I was just hitting my stride, you know.'

'And you wanted to hit it a bit more. Well, there'll be other times. Remember that. As for myself, there aren't many pleasant tasks in this job, but telling Sascha and Sadie they're free to go will be one of them. I'll leave Chomsky to you.'

As he blew smoke up into the air duct I told myself he was right.

It wasn't until a few seconds later and we were outside that Dingus's last words registered.

'What *did* you do with Chomsky in the end?'

'Everything we could to get rid of him,' he told me, spitting tobacco juice onto the sidewalk. 'But he said he wasn't going anywhere unless Sascha and Sadie were going with him. And he said it extremely forcefully indeed.'

I chuckled. 'So you don't want to give him the good news yourself?'

'Oh no,' Dingus said, shaking his head and getting his ears in a flap. 'Definitely not. I get the impression he doesn't like me very much.'

Following him back to the station, Dingus arranged for an officer to take me up to Chomsky.

Unlike the last time I saw him he was strangely cowed, all the fight gone out of him. As I told him what we now knew, he took a spindly cigarette from his pocket with a trembling paw. Stepping forward, the officer who'd come up with me lit it for him. But he didn't take a drag from it until I'd finished speaking.

'I couldn't be certain, you know,' he said after sucking the cigarette for several seconds. 'It hurts me to say that. Sasha *does* have a temper. After you brought me home from Kowalski's –' Rubbing at the cut above his eye, he shook his head. 'But murder? I was pretty sure she *couldn't* have killed him, but what if –?' He looked up at me with his large, sad eyes, the brown gunk beneath the left one glistening. 'You've seen what she's like, Spriteman – she wouldn't last five minutes in the jug.'

'So you tried to get us to think it was you.'

'I thought if I took your attention away from Sascha and Sadie you'd find something in the meantime to prove it was someone else. I should've guessed they wouldn't have been able to keep it to themselves if they thought they'd done it. Good thing you were on the ball, huh?'

'Come on,' I said. 'Let's go and see them.' Sucking the last of the nicotine from his cigarette, he stood up.

When the elevator opened onto the first floor, everyone was there waiting for us. Walking quickly towards Sascha, Chomsky mumbled something to her that I didn't catch before putting his arms around her and holding her tightly. Returning the gesture, she began to sob.

Turning away, I went over to Sadie and the Mouse who were talking close by, the Mouse towering over her despite being seated.

'Okay?' I asked Sadie.

'I am now,' she said, smiling up at me. It was a nice smile – for a Goat, anyway.

'Let's go then,' I said, smiling back at her.

Like last time, the Mouse and I took Sadie in my car. Not surprisingly, Sascha wanted to be with her brother and went with the Lieutenant. Tailing them the whole way, I watched as they chatted in the back of Dingus's car, barely stopping for breath.

'Thank god that's all over,' Sadie said at one point. 'Oh, to get back to normal.'

'Hmm,' I replied. Thankfully the Mouse, never stuck for something to say, kept the conversation going.

Pulling up in Montcrieff Terrace the Mouse helped her out of the car while I went over to talk to Chomsky.

'Well, I guess that's it then, if Bouchard isn't coming back,' he said.

'I guess so. Unless you want me to keep looking for her?'

'What's the point? Chances are it was Moseley who killed Gino and he got his punishment. As for Lady Muck, she'll get what's coming to her. I'm sure of it.'

'Yeah, maybe you're right. The thing is, if *I* get her there'd be a trail. You could see justice done. But the chances are if somebody *else* gets her –' Shrugging, I let the sentence hang.

Thinking about it for a second, he shrugged back. 'Like I give a Rat's ass,' he said, turning towards the Pawnbroker's. 'See ya later, Spriteman. And thanks. I'll be in touch.' Just before the door closed behind him I thought I heard a telephone ringing.

With that I went over to the Mouse, who now was talking with the Lieutenant by his car. Opening my mouth, I was just about to tell him to go home and get some shuteye when the door of the Pawnbroker's opened and Sascha appeared.

'Someone on the phone for you, Lieutenant,' she said. 'It sounds important.' Looking at his watch, Dingus pulled a face before following Sascha inside.

'Okay Linus,' I said, running my paw along the side of the Lieutenant's car, 'that's us. See you in the morning. Actually, make that afternoon. Technically it's morning now. Go home and get some sleep.'

'Well, I'll try. But it's funny, I don't feel tired now.'

'No. Me neither.'

'Really? According to the Lieutenant it sounds like you've had quite a night of it.'

'Yeah. I have. Just like the old days.' Smiling back at me awkwardly he didn't reply. 'Still, there'll be others. G'night.'

At some point during our conversation it had started raining again, peppering us with large, fur-flattening drops. Preferring a shower in the comfort of my own bathroom rather than out on the street, I dashed for my car. I was maybe three steps from it when the door of the Pawnbroker's burst open and Dingus emerged, rubbing a paw across his face.

'What's wrong, Lieutenant?' the Mouse asked.

'That was Officer Mulcahy, calling from the station,' he said. 'He's been trying to get hold of me since we left, but earlier today my radio finally – I kept telling them I needed a new one – anyway, someone just called from the hospital where they took Vincent. They went in to check on her and the officer who should've been standing outside wasn't there. They found him in Vincent's room unconscious on the floor, but there was no sign of her. The officer's gun and keys were missing and his car wasn't in the parking lot – Benji? What is it?'

Smiling so hard it hurt my face, I took the remaining three steps to my car and dug out my keys.

'Benji, what is it?' he shouted as I climbed inside. 'Where are you going?' Slamming the door and gunning the engine, I swung the car round in the road, tires shrieking, and tore out of Montcrieff Terrace with the smile still plastered across my face.

There was only one reason Vincent would go to such lengths to escape: to get to Mimi. And she'd only do that if she knew where Mimi was hiding out. And now I thought I knew too, the realisation suddenly slamming into my head with the force of a charging Rhino. Vincent had been smart about covering it up when she blurted it out, but not smart enough: where this case was concerned, it seemed I still had a little stride left to hit. So bombing along the rain-slicked streets I drove as fast as I could in the general direction of Turnbull Street and a certain jewellers situated there in particular.

Janklow's.

29.

Hurtling down every road and byway, through every junction and red light, the world was reduced to little more than a series of neon smudges in the darkness as I headed for the outskirts of town, each blink of colour reminding me of the jewels on a dagger I hadn't seen, reminding me what it was capable of, driving me on, pushing my paw down even harder on the gas until the engine bellowed in complaint.

Eventually forcing myself to slow down enough for the *clump-clump, clump-clump* of the windshield wipers to be heard, I peered through the rain-smeared glass looking for signs for Turnbull Street, a street I vaguely recalled driving down on one of my evening jaunts months earlier. Failing to see anything I recognised, I realised I must have come at it last time from a different direction; then, just as I was starting to worry I wouldn't find it I saw a sign up ahead. Taking a sharp left, I emerged on Turnbull Street, a long, tree-lined street full of townhouses with an almost unbroken line of top-of-the-range cars parked along both kerbs. Both sides of the road free of traffic, I increased my pace, looking for anything that resembled a storefront. And then, right at the end of the road, blocking it off in much the same way

Mimi's Salon blocked off the end of Montcrieff Terrace, was a flat-roofed detached building, on top of which was a discreet sign, glowing in a pale, creamy light: JANKLOW'S – JEWELLERS OF DISTINCTION. Its front door was open; and not so much parked out front as dumped there was an empty squad car.

Seeing nothing else now except the car and the door, I slammed the gas pedal down to the floor, almost halving the distance in an instant, hoping that I wasn't too late, hoping that I still had a chance to close the case; and as these thoughts formed I saw the front door of the jewellers creep open further, almost in slow motion, and a figure appear in the doorway–

Before I could see who it was I was blinded by a bright yellow flash, at the centre of which was something resembling a large, scythe-like blade sweeping towards me. Yanking the steering wheel hard left, I somehow managed to swerve around it, my tires skidding and shrieking on the road's wet surface; but I was going too fast, and the yellow flash was replaced by the dark, crouching shapes of parked cars and the liquid green of trees on the opposite side of the road. Wrestling the wheel to the right, it was more good luck than judgement that saw me avoiding a badly-parked saloon by a matter of inches and bump up on the sidewalk, barely missing the tree to my right; but bad luck that saw me hurtling at breakneck speed towards the townhouses. Screaming, I stamped on the brakes, still wrenching the wheel to the right, willing the car to change course, willing it back onto the road, then miraculously seeing the road between two trees only to have it disappear behind one of them, its gnarled trunk and bright green leaves filling my windshield until nothing else existed and there was an almighty *bang* and I was thrown forwards and a second *bang* as my view of the tree momentarily broke apart in a million tiny pieces before reappearing and disappearing again as I shot up through it into the darkness surrounded by small chips of light into a sky full of brighter lights, which too disappeared as I began my descent into a different kind of darkness, one where a scythe-like blade was sweeping towards me, and where sometimes you had to face your fears head on–

And as that thought struck me a little scene began playing in my head, one where a Toucan was silhouetted against the staircase of an old apartment block with its huge beak lunging at something but I couldn't see what it was or think what it reminded me of – only now, with my mind speeding almost as fast as my body towards the ground, I thought I did know; and then something else popped into my head: maybe the Tuke hadn't been *lunging* at anything; maybe it'd just been–

Before I had a chance to finish the thought I smacked into the ground so hard I thought I was going to break it, leaving me little more than a lump of hot, stinging pain lying face down in the driving rain, a lump that didn't much care about footsteps or murmuring voices or being grabbed under the arms and dragged face-first through a puddle or being roughly lifted off the ground, only really caring when the pain became too much to bear after smacking into something hard a second time and I couldn't feel anything any more.

30.

Waking up shivering and in agony I looked around, realised where I was and who I was with and felt marginally worse. Getting a look at myself as we passed a streetlight, I saw I was squashed into my seat at an awkward angle and that my fur was covered with small pieces of glass cutting into my skin.

'I seem to be bleeding all over your upholstery,' I said, a wave of dizziness and nausea coursing through me.

'Forget about it,' Vincent said lightly, 'it's not mine. Not a bad old motor, though – for a while there I thought your friends were going to catch me, but between us –' slapping the steering wheel, she smiled – 'we managed to outrun them.'

Speeding along I felt every little bump in the road, each taking my breath, so it took me a while to ask the obvious question. 'Where are we going?' I eventually gasped.

'Janklow's,' Vincent said.

When I scowled I found even that hurt. 'But we were just there. That's where I –' shuddering, I pushed the thought aside.

She shook her head. 'Uh-huh. When I heard Mimi

talking about Janklow's I assumed she'd meant the jewellers. It turns out I was wrong.'

'It seems I was wrong too,' I said. 'About you. The way you suddenly became a basket-case in the interview room? That was a neat trick.' Going over another uneven stretch of road, my insides convulsed again.

'I wondered if you'd figure that out,' Vincent said, a smile coming to her lips. 'But once I knew what she'd done to Marv I was determined I was going to get her, one way or the other.' Tensing, she gripped the steering wheel tight. 'But at that moment I couldn't think where she might be.'

'And realising you were going to be in the station for the foreseeable future you pulled the stunt with the business card to buy you a bit of thinking time. Only by the time we came back from Wareham, Krukowski & Yang's you still hadn't worked it out.'

'Every time I tried all I could see was Marv's face,' she said. 'Besides, I didn't get much of a chance with the Doctor hovering around. I thought maybe if you started asking me questions again it might help me remember something. So I told the doc' I needed to speak to you about it all. If nothing else answering your questions might take some of the heat off me.'

'And then when we asked you to name names you hit upon Janklow's.'

'I just started saying the first things that came into my head,' she said almost dreamily. 'I suppose the name stuck because when Mimi spoke to him on the phone she always took the calls in private. On top of that Marv bought her a jewel-handled dagger from there once. Strange, how things stick in your mind.' She glanced across at me but I didn't meet her gaze. 'You never did say how Marv died, Mr Spriteman.'

I tried locking down my expression but apparently wasn't quick enough; unnerved by the way she was choking the steering wheel again I said, 'The problem was once you'd said "Janklow's" you had to cover it up straight away. So you pretended to be strung out on drugs so we wouldn't take anything that you'd said seriously.'

'Well, we had just been talking about Mimi's plants a few seconds before. And having seen what it's done to some of her girls it was easy enough to copy the symptoms. So that's what I did.' *Only I followed up what you said anyway and somehow here I am,* I nearly said, but thought better of it.

Leaving it a few seconds, I asked, 'This other place of Janklow's – how can you be sure Mimi'll be there?'

'Because that's where Janklow told me she is, hiding away in a little place he has out of town. And it's amazing how truthful a Guinea Pig can be when he's got a gun barrel jammed in his ear. Before you ask, he's not in a position to warn her I'm on my way – not after what I just did to him and the telephone.' Before I had a chance to ask anything, we went over what felt like a huge crater in the road. Lurching forward, I squelched against the dashboard briefly before collapsing back into my seat in another wave of dizziness and nausea.

'You know, I could really do with going to the hospital,' I managed to gasp once I'd got some of my breath back.

'Oh, we can't do that, Mr Spriteman,' Vincent said briskly. 'We've got to go and see Mimi.'

'A little while ago there's nothing I'd have liked more,' I started. 'But now –'

'But you *have* to come, Mr Spriteman,' she said, imploring me like a child. 'If you don't, who's going to hear her confessing to Marv's murder? Okay – tell you what – after I've killed Mimi if you *still* need to go to the hospital I'll take you then. How does that sound?' Turning to face me, she smiled brightly.

If I'd had any doubts about her being mad before I certainly didn't now. Luckily I didn't have long to think about it as a few seconds later we rumbled over another pothole in the road and a sharp bolt of pain passed through me when I hit the dashboard, causing me to lose consciousness.

31.

Four seconds or four hours later, a paw was on my shoulder, shaking me vigorously.

'Wake up sleepyhead,' a voice whispered in my ear. 'We're here.'

Opening my eyes, the first thing I saw was the gun pointed in my face.

'Right,' Vincent said, moving the gun back a fraction. 'Out.'

I tried to oblige, but my body ached so much I could barely move. Losing patience, she hauled me out of the car and onto the sidewalk, slamming the door shut behind me. Pain and cold air grabbed at my lungs, making me gasp. Squinting through the now torrential rain, it looked like we were about two-thirds of the way along a straight, narrow road, at the end of which sat a solitary house in darkness.

'Start moving,' Vincent said, jabbing the gun into my back, narrowly missing what felt like a cracked rib.

Hobbling forwards, I had to take it slower than I would have liked because of the pain, half expecting her to jab the gun in further at any second. 'How are you going to get in?' I said, hoping to keep her mind from such thoughts.

'How are *we* going to get in, you mean. There's a spare key under a plant pot in the back garden, fourth paving slab along.'

Perhaps finally realising I wasn't in any state to run off and get help, Vincent stepped ahead of me to open the garden gate, keeping her eye on me as she did so. The gun pointed at my chest, she waved me through before closing the gate behind us. Then, taking up her position behind me once more, the gun firmly wedged into my back, she frogmarched me along the side of the house to the rear of the property.

While Vincent grubbed around among the paving slabs looking for the key, I took the opportunity to glance around and try and get my breath back. Unlike the front of the house all the windows had their curtains drawn; however, in a gap between them in one of the upstairs windows a faint light was visible. As I looked at it I heard a noise to my right. Turning, I saw Vincent getting up off the ground, gazing at the small silver key in her paw.

'Under the plant pot, fourth paving slab along, just like he said,' she smiled. But as she gazed at it I found my attention was focused on her other paw, the one holding the gun, reminding me of my own – not that I could get to it. But if I picked the right moment when I could–

Caught up in the idea I almost jumped as Vincent strode past me to unlock the door before falling in behind me. Giving me a sharp dig in the back, she nudged me over the threshold.

With my eyes already fully adjusted to the dark, I looked around at what was a fairly large and sparsely-furnished kitchen. On the stove the dregs from a nearly-empty coffee pot wafted their stink towards me. It was a smell I usually loved, but at that moment it made me want to retch. Trying my best not to, we shuffled past the stove over to a closed door on the other side of the room. A few inches away Vincent breathed into my ear: 'Open it. Slowly.'

Despite the discomfort it caused I took a deep breath, released it and grabbed the handle, easing the door open as gently as I could, all the while waiting for the inevitable creak, but amazingly, none came: not until the gap was wide enough for us both to get through and a death-throes groan sounded throughout the house.

Most animals in that situation would have waited for a few seconds to see if they'd got away with it, but not Vincent, who took it as a cue for action. Using me as a shield, she pushed me through the doorway into the hall, the staircase to our right. Near the top I sensed movement through the banister rail, saw Hagen crouching there, his bulging eyes glowing in the darkness, his teeth bared in hatred, the gun aimed at my face, the hairs in my ears frying with the blast from the gunshots–

Instinctively raising my paws to my head as Hagen slumped forward, almost knocking the gun from Vincent's paw as I did so, I watched as he tumbled heavily down the stairs before thudding to the bottom in a bloody heap. Before his limbs had even stopped moving a snarling Vincent shoved me aside, kicking the body away from the stairs; and, just when I thought she couldn't shock me further, fired two more bullets into the corpse before turning back to face me.

'I don't know if you meant to do that,' Vincent hissed, her ice-blue eyes piercing the darkness, 'but just remember I still have two bullets left.' Getting behind me again she jammed the gun hard into my side, this time into one of my cracked ribs, the needle sharp pain making me cry out. 'Now,' she growled. 'Upstairs.'

Gritting my teeth I stumbled past Hagen's body and made my way awkwardly up the stairs, thinking I was going to collapse at any second, each step harder than the last. Eventually getting to the top and seeing the three closed doors ahead, I nearly cried out with relief at the opportunity to stop. Not caring what Vincent might do to me, I bent down and clamped my paws on my knees and tried to suck in as much air as my damaged body would allow in a series of ragged breaths. Beside me, Vincent stood breathing heavily through her nose, one paw squeezed tight into a fist, the other tight around the gun, her breathing getting heavier and louder until a voice called out from behind the middle door:

'For heaven's sake, stop all the panting and come in.'

Mimi.

'You heard her,' Vincent rasped, prodding me with the gun again. 'Move.'

Fumbling with the knob, I tried not to think about the dagger that might be waiting for me on the other side of the door. Swallowing hard, I gently pushed the door open; and when no dagger came, I looked quickly around the room.

It appeared to be a decent size but it was so cluttered it was hard to tell, with a small cot under the window and a sideboard and large closet taking up the lion's share of the space, the only light coming from a small lamp on a table beside the wall a few feet away. Like our previous meetings, Mimi hid herself away in the gloom; but I managed to pick her out just beyond the arc of the lamplight, over to the left.

'So Aidy didn't finish you off after all,' she purred. 'He couldn't even do that one simple thing for me. Still, it sounds like he paid the price for it. And with four bullets, too – you must be a lousy shot.'

'I think the first one did the trick,' I told her. 'But it wasn't me who shot him.'

'No?' she purred again.

'No,' Vincent said, stepping into the room and closing the door behind her, 'I did.'

For the briefest of moments Mimi looked less than self-assured, but quickly regained her composure. 'Well,' she cooed, seemingly unconcerned about the gun being pointed at her, 'look what the Cat dragged in.'

For upwards of a minute they stared at each other, neither one blinking, although it was apparent that Vincent was having the most trouble keeping her emotions in check, the gun wavering slightly in her paw.

To my immense surprise it was Mimi who blinked first. 'Impressive,' she said with a smile, raising her paws in defeat. 'But I don't imagine you came all this way just to stare at me. Then again, maybe you did.'

'Oh, you know why I'm here,' Vincent said through clenched teeth. 'But before I do it you're going to admit a few things.'

'Am I?' Mimi said, almost grinning now. 'You mean about dear old Marvin! Well, I'm sure you know now what *really* happened to him… what can I say? He was in my way, so I got rid of him. Simple as that.'

Laughing like she didn't have a care in the world, she shrugged. 'Oh Caro, after all I've done for you. But, if this is how you want it to be you could at least even up the odds a bit by getting rid of the gun – unless you don't think you can beat me without it, that is.'

'I can beat you all right,' Vincent said with conviction. 'Gun or no gun.'

'Well, in that case throw it into the corner and we can have ourselves a fair fight.'

After barely a second's pause Vincent tossed the gun over to the right, towards the back of the room.

'That's better,' Mimi said, a sly grin breaking out on her face. 'Now we have ourselves a fair fight, don't we? The two of you –' casting a contemptuous glance in my direction, she slipped a long-bladed knife from the back of her pants, its tip catching the light from the lamp like a lit match, 'against me and my gift from darling Marvin. And you know what? I'm going to do to both of you what I did to him.'

If there was ever a right time to grab my gun that was it. Unfortunately I never even got close. Seeing the dagger that killed Falconetti, Vincent went crazy, throwing herself at Mimi and sending me flying over to the right into the table and lamp, both crashing to the floor, yanking the cord from the lamp in the process and plunging the room into near darkness. All thoughts of the gun forgotten I lay there in agony, panting as my eyes adjusted to the murk whilst to my left Mimi and Vincent rolled around on the floor spitting and screeching and pulling out fistfuls of fur, the dagger no longer in Mimi's possession, lying just a few feet away. Raising herself into a half-sitting position, Vincent slapped Mimi hard across the face and made a lunge for the knife; but before she got there Mimi sprang up and pinned Vincent to the ground, shoving one of her arms up her back; and, with the other trapped beneath her, Mimi reached forward and grabbed the dagger, holding the blade to Vincent's throat.

'Weak,' Mimi hissed, pressing the tip of the blade into Vincent's flesh. 'All of you. Weak and stupid.'

Unable to help her as she struggled and knowing I didn't have long before I passed out again, I did the only thing I could do: talk.

'You may be right,' I wheezed, not even sure my

voice would carry to them, 'but if we are you're not much better. For all your money and trinkets you're still the same desperate animal you were when you latched onto Falconetti, still rolling around on the floor and scrabbling in the dirt. Because despite it all, despite all your achievements Miss Bouchard, you're still her: *you're still Betty.*'

Hissing like a piece of frying meat, she raised her eyes and fixed me with a stare so terrifying it almost shocked my body back to life. But it worked. Momentarily loosening her grip on Vincent, she was able to move her head round just enough to bite down on the arm holding the dagger. Sinking her teeth in deep, the blade clattered to the floor; but before she could gain the advantage Mimi let go of the grip she had on Vincent's arm, instead grabbing a fistful of fur at the back of her head, causing Vincent to release her grip on Mimi's arm; and with incredible strength began pulling her away from the knife, forcing Vincent backwards on top of her and sending them both clattering into the closet behind them, the dagger forgotten once again as they howled and screeched and tore at each other, careering off the walls and clutter. With little left for me to do but try and get out of the way, I just about managed to drag myself up to a sitting position before dizziness got the better of me, the spinning room bringing on wave after wave of nausea; closing my eyes to try and stop the dizziness, I felt myself sinking into sleep, a lovely black pool of emptiness; only to have it shrink away from me when I sensed movement close by and my eyelids flickered open.

Heavily bloodied and missing great swatches of fur, Mimi was crawling across the floor towards me – or rather towards the dagger – but standing over her, equally bloodied and bedraggled, was Vincent; and in her right paw was something better than any knife: the gun she'd thrown down earlier. Enjoying her advantage, Vincent let Mimi inch across the floor for a few seconds like some half-dead fly she was about to swat until she was maybe a foot from the dagger; then, taking a deep breath, she raised the gun and aimed it at the back of Mimi's head, squeezing the trigger almost to the point of no return – only to toss the gun away from her with a smile before dropping to the floor. And with one knee jarred against Mimi's spine, she reached across her prone body for the jewel-handled dagger, its stones sparkling and winking impossibly at me like a Cat's eyes in the darkness as my own dimmed.

Barely conscious now, I imagined I heard a wailing, siren-like sound in the distance – another hallucination – and wanted nothing more than to sleep, but knew I had to make one last effort to do something; yet even shuffling myself round to the left slightly proved too much and I lost my balance, flopping back onto the floor with what felt like a solid block of pain in my side too large to be one of my ribs, my eyes slipping shut in the darkness; and as they did I thought I knew what that pain was: my gun, tucked away in my inside pocket. But digging my paw into the pocket despite the agony I knew it would cause, I came back empty; confused, I tried the other pocket, wondering if my muddled senses had got it wrong; but the gun wasn't there either. Then, wondering if it'd dropped from my pocket when I fell against the table I started scrabbling blindly on the floor around me, but again nothing, filling me with panic that I'd lost it earlier in the evening, perhaps when Hagen knocked me out cold, or maybe before that *when he threw me spine first into that metal post...* hearing that bell-like chime in my head as clearly as when it happened, I groaned. My last faint chance gone, all I could do was lay there in the dark, listening to the hideous struggle going on barely a few feet away and the other noises that suddenly threatened to engulf it – the siren wails, the drumming of thunder rushing beneath me, quickly followed by violent pounding a few feet away above me:

'Police – open up!'

But still the pounding continued and no-one came, each blow heavier than the last, becoming so strong that I seemed to feel each one. Opening my mouth I tried to call out, but my feeble effort was blotted out by a chilling feral yell on my left.

'Christ, we need to get in there now! Is it locked?'

'I don't think so – something's blocking the way.'

'Well get it out of the way!'

And so the blows continued and still no-one came because it was my body blocking the door and I was too weak to do anything about it, too weak to call out, too weak to feel the pain as the blows became more frantic and started inching the door inwards, nudging me ever closer to the dreadful, hissing cacophony of noise that now seemed only a matter of inches away and which culminated in a terrible, clogged, watery cry followed by a sickeningly heavy thud onto the floor, at which point the door finally burst open and the last thing I heard were the short, ragged gasps of whoever lay beside me trying desperately to cling to life...

Three: Future – ?

32.

'Well,' Taki said, 'that's us.'

Looking up from my desk, I saw Taki and the Mouse standing in the doorway, Taki wearing her full-length fake fur buttoned up to the neck, the Mouse wrapped in the incredibly long scarf his mother had knitted him the winter before. Laid end to end, I reckoned you could have stretched it from my window to the one on the fourth floor opposite, like some woolly telephone wire.

'There's talk of snow tonight,' Taki continued. 'You don't want to get snowed in. Could be a difficult journey home if you're not – well, I'll see you in the morning. Don't be long,' she whispered to the Mouse.

Stepping over the threshold, the Mouse eyed me like something in a petri dish.

'Everything okay?' I asked, smiling up at him.

'Yeah, sure. Mr S – Are you – are you *sure* y–'

'I'm fine,' I told him. 'Just fine.'

'Well, I'd better get going,' he said eventually. 'I told Taki I'd give her a lift to the bus depot. Best not keep her waiting.'

'Quite right too. Goodnight.'

'Yeah,' he said, eyeing me carefully before casting a glance over at the pile of untouched papers on my desk, 'g'night.'

Since starting back, this little performance had become a nightly fixture – he'd ask how I was, I'd tell him I was fine, he wouldn't believe me. Part of it I felt sure was guilt – guilt that he hadn't been able to stop what'd happened to me after I roared out of Montcrieff Terrace. Not that he had anything to be guilty about. But when I tried to broach the topic his ears would go bright pink and he'd change the subject. Then of course there was his report, which I'd been putting off reading since I came back, and which he wanted my opinion on. It wasn't as if I didn't know what it was going to say – I was fairly sure what it was going to say, that was part of the problem – but every time I went to pick it up I found that I wasn't ready to relive the experience in forensic detail, further leading the Mouse to question whether I'd come back too soon.

Getting up gingerly from my desk a few minutes later, I went over to the window to find that Taki had been right about the snow. Soothed by the swirling flakes, I watched them until they began to settle on the windowsill then reluctantly turned away, catching sight of my reflection in the glass as I did so, seeing a worn-out feline with bent whiskers and sunken eyes, framed not by flakes of snow but small, glass-like chips of light. Blinking the image away I hurried towards the coat rack, nudging the Mouse's report close to the edge of the desk on the way. Putting on my hat and coat, I stood with my claw on the light switch, looking back at the report, the edges of the topmost papers hanging over the side of the desk.

Tomorrow, I told myself. *I'll read it tomorrow. Or maybe the day after.*

Flicking the switch, I set out for home.

*

After the events of that night I was out cold for two days, and for two days after that I remembered little, the Mouse apparently staying by my side in the hospital the whole time. Once I was fully able to understand, I learned that I had two broken ribs, three fractured ribs, two very badly bruised arms and enough glass cuts to make me look like I'd been attacked by several Octopuses with flick-knives. But it wasn't until the Lieutenant came by to visit and managed to persuade the Mouse to go home for a while that I found out what happened after I finally passed out at Janklow's.

He said it was quite a scene. Charging inside once they finally got the door open, the cops found what they thought were dead two bodies lying face down on the floor – yours truly, and a few feet beyond me, Mimi – and crouched over us like some demented gargoyle with a dagger in her paw dripping blood onto the floorboards was Vincent. Eventually prising the dagger away from her and getting her out of there, the cops turned their attention to the stiffs only to find that one of them was still alive, with nary a knife wound on him. The same couldn't be said for Mimi, Vincent having cut her throat from ear to ear in pretty much the same way Mimi had cut Falconetti's.

It wasn't all doom and gloom in the hospital, however. Besides the Mouse I had plenty of visitors – Taki and the Lieutenant showed up when they could, along with Sadie, who seemed to be recovering from her ordeal, and Harvey turned up one afternoon, followed in the evening by Laurence on his way to the Adelphi, armed with an expensive box of chocolates and the biggest bunch of carnations I'd ever seen – evidently, the winning streak I'd set in motion was still going strong;

at least, for one of us. But undoubtedly my best day for visitors was when the delegation of Squirrels from the forest turned up after hitching a ride to town on the back of a truck, causing no end of mayhem scurrying up and down the wards until the Doctors cleared them out with brooms.

And then there was my visit from the Chomsky's.

'Well, I'll be,' Chomsky said as he dragged a couple of chairs over to the bed. 'When that Mouse of yours said you were back in the land of the living I could hardly believe it. Not that I thought you were going to – anyway, if I had a beer with me I'd drink to your health, that's all I'm saying. Even if I have given it up,' he added, casting a bitter glance in Sascha's direction.

'We'll have a small glass of sherry on Sunday and drink to Mr Spriteman's health then,' Sascha said primly. 'Now, I know you boys have business to discuss so I'll leave you to it. In the meantime, I'll go and get us some coffee...' Humming merrily to herself, she shuffled away.

'Sherry on Sunday my ass,' Chomsky grumbled once she was safely out of earshot. 'I'd rather drink my own – well, I'd better not say. Apparently my language is something else I need to moderate. Anyhow, got something for you.' Reaching into his pocket he pulled out a check and handed it over. 'God knows you've earned it.'

'Thanks.'

For a few minutes we chatted of this and that, but like most animals visiting someone laid up in hospital Chomsky ran out of things to say. It was only after I asked him how business was that he realised he had something else to tell me after all.

'If what happened yesterday is anything to go by business could be looking up,' he told me, rubbing his paws together with glee. 'That sign Bouchard's thugs vandalised? Well, yesterday I sold it.'

'You *sold* it? But it was worthless as it was. Who'd you sell it to, someone looking for offensive firewood?'

'No, that's the beauty of it; they wanted it as it was. I mean, how they *found out* about it, I've no idea – god knows how these things get around – but these two mutts showed up, saying they worked in manure – you know, for gardens, stuff like that – so the graffiti on the sign was perfect. As one of them put it to me, the sign works in two ways – it tells you exactly what's on offer – crap – *and* it adds a touch of humour to the situation, so –'

I held the laugh in for as long as I could knowing the pain it would cause, but it was no good – in the end it had to come out. I only stopped laughing after Chomsky called a nurse over and she gave me something to calm me down. On his way out, the look he gave me suggested I was crazy.

I swear I cracked another rib laughing.

Just before I came out of hospital I heard a report on the radio about Mimi Bouchard's funeral, one of the biggest the city had seen since The Terror and which was apparently very well attended, presumably by her many rivals who wanted to make sure she was really gone. All in all it sounded like quite an elaborate affair, with a Horse-drawn carriage and a dozen or so professional mourners wailing away in time with a brass band. The very idea that she'd even considered the possibility of dying surprised me. One couple interviewed, seemingly unaware of who she was or how she'd died, put forward the opinion that it was refreshing to see someone celebrating their life in such a fashion. No mention was made in the report of Falconetti or Moseley or Hagen or Wareham or Dash

Norman or Osterlein or the girls that Mimi used, or anyone else she had in her clutches – myself included. But it was Vincent who I felt most sorry for. Following her fight to the death with Mimi, she was seen by a doctor and taken straight to the nearest mental institution, where she's likely to remain indefinitely; this time, she definitely *wasn't* faking it. And all because she'd wanted a little excitement in her life. And, thanks to Mimi Bouchard, that's exactly what she got.

Boy, did she.

A couple of days and several inches of snow later, while Taki was out to lunch and the Mouse was on a tailing job, I finally kept my promise to myself and read the Mouse's report – or more specifically, the section dealing with the events following my departure from Montcrieff Terrace. Skimming past Dingus's decision to follow me figuring I might be onto something and having the Mouse drive in his car because it was quicker than the Lieutenant's, I was surprised to learn that they caught sight of me relatively quickly; and Dingus, noting the general direction I was driving and recalling our conversation with Vincent earlier, realised I must be heading for Janklow's. They almost got there before me too – Dingus, having worked the area before on another case, said he knew a few short cuts; but unfortunately the narrow side street they took which would have brought them out halfway up Turnbull Street was blocked off at the end by a badly-parked car.

Taking a couple of deep breaths, I read the Mouse's account of what he saw next:

'...*deciding it would make more sense to continue on foot than to turn back, we made our way past the errant vehicle onto Turnbull Street itself just as Mr Spriteman was driving* past, travelling at speed towards the jewellers, when his progress was impeded by a large-beaked yellow Budgerigar stepping out between the trees and cars on the right-hand side of the road and straight in front of Mr Spriteman's vehicle. Swerving left and narrowly avoiding the creature, Mr Spriteman's car careered wildly over to the opposite side of the road, along which were several trees and numerous parked cars; but thanks to some highly-skilled manoeuvring on Mr Spriteman's part a second collision was avoided as he managed to angle the car between them and up onto the sidewalk, where I lost sight of it due to my position on the road; but with the car still going at tremendous speed in spite of Mr Spriteman's obvious attempts to stop it, a crash of some kind seemed inevitable. Too far away to do anything to stop the accident itself, I nevertheless began to run up Turnbull Street with the aim of being at the crash site as soon as possible, only to be stopped dead in my tracks by a terrific thud ahead on my left followed by the sight of Mr Spriteman's body flying through the trees in a shower of glass fragments before landing face down on the road not far from the jewellers and just ahead of a badly-parked police car out front.

Stunned as I was by the sight of Mr Spriteman lying in the road, I failed to notice the appearance of Ms Vincent on the scene, evidently making her way from the jewellers back towards the squad car. Finally gathering some of my wits, I once again began running up Turnbull Street towards Mr Spriteman; but before any real progress was made I was halted by the sight of Ms Vincent brandishing the gun she'd stolen from the police officer at the hospital and the wild look in her eyes that stated she wouldn't think twice about using it. Reluctantly backing away, as did the Lieutenant who was now almost level with me, we could only watch as Ms Vincent made her way over to Mr Spriteman, the gun still trained on us, and, after crouching down beside him for a second and appearing to speak to him she tucked the gun into her pants, grabbed him *under the arms and roughly dragged him across the road towards the squad car a few feet away, only stopping once she appeared to reach the passenger-side door on the other side of the vehicle. Being on the 'wrong side' of the car as I was and with my view further obscured by the driving rain, I was unable to properly see what happened next; but somehow and with a strength I wouldn't have believed possible in such a small feline, Ms Vincent managed to drag and lift Mr Spriteman's lifeless body into the passenger seat before running around to the driver's side, gunning the engine, turning the car around and shooting straight past us back out of Turnbull Street.'*

Having to stop for a few seconds because my paws were shaking the papers so badly, I took a dozen or so deep breaths before reading on and learning how Dingus and the Mouse had raced back to their car to follow Vincent and how they'd almost caught her before she gave them the slip following what the Mouse described as 'an almost suicidal piece of driving'. After that and with Dingus's radio still on the blink they'd had no choice but to put a call through to the station from a phone booth giving the general direction Vincent was heading and getting every available squad car out looking for her. Taking yet another deep breath I dropped the report on the desk, the pages fanning out to cover most of the surface.

Coming back from his tailing job later on, the Mouse looked at the papers sprawled across my desk then expectantly at me.

'Very good,' I said, keeping things as business-like as I could. 'Your comments about my skills as a driver are a touch on the generous side but otherwise it's fine. One question though: what happened to the Budgie?'

Putting his paw up to his face, red spots came up under his fur.

'I – I don't know,' he said, shocked. 'With everything else going on I never thought about him. He didn't even try to *help*. I'll – I'll redo the report – I can't believe I missed it –'

'Forget it,' I said as he reached towards the desk. 'It doesn't make any difference anyway. Chances are he was just some lush on a late-night bender who didn't even know what happened next. Or maybe he did, saw the cop car and waddled off back between the trees. Either way, it changes nothing. And neither, Linus, could you. You have to trust me on that.'

'But we need to find him –'

'No, we don't. It was just one of those things. Wrong place and wrong time. Okay?'

'Well,' he said, not entirely convinced, 'if you're sure.'

'I'm sure,' I told him. 'See you tomorrow.'

'Right. Well, bye Mr S.' Giving me a final questioning look, he hurried out of the office.

How long I sat there mulling things over after the Mouse left I don't know, but by the time I'd finished I was sitting in the dark. As I'd thought earlier, the report didn't tell me anything I didn't already know or suspect – like the scythe I thought I'd seen in the road turning out to be little more than that damned Bird's beak or how it was I ended up in Vincent's car on my way to Janklow's – it was more what I *thought* it said about my state of mind in the first place that bothered me. And *that* still needed to be confirmed. So, grabbing my hat and coat I locked up the office and took myself across town to a particular old apartment block; and after pausing to look at its metal staircase for a few seconds, made my way to the door.

Thankfully I didn't have to start pressing buzzers at random to get in. As I approached an elderly Sheepdog was coming out, and seeing me struggling through the snow held the door open for me.

'Thanks,' I said. 'Um, actually, you might be able to help me. I'm looking for a Toucan who lives here.'

'Toucan? That'll be Todhunter,' the Sheepdog replied. 'Apartment thirty-nine. You'll know you're getting close 'cos you'll hear his kids squawking. Nice enough though.'

Taking the elevator up to the third floor, I looked for apartment thirty-nine. Sure enough, three doors before I got there I heard kids' voices up ahead.

Knocking on the door louder than I intended, I stood back and waited.

I seemed to be standing there a long time before I heard a voice yelling on the other side of the door for quiet. Finally the door began to open and a large, shell-like beak started to fill my vision. As it did, my breathing got heavier and my insides began to tighten.

Standing before me in the door frame, he looked me up and down. 'Yeah?'

Not silhouetted against the staircase, he just looked like any other six-foot high Tuke, but I still had to suppress a shudder. Barely able to look him in the eye and stumbling over my words, I eventually managed to say: 'I'm sorry to bother you – um, we haven't met, and this is going to sound like a silly question and you might not even remember – but four, five weeks ago did you have a heavy cold?'

After looking at me like I'd escaped from the local booby-hatch for a few seconds the Tuke thought about it. 'As a matter of fact, yeah, I did,' he said, rubbing the tip of his beak with a wing. 'How the hell did you know that?'

'Oh, I saw you sneezing out beside your fire escape one night, that's all. It's not important. Anyway, thanks for your time.' Before he had a chance to quiz me further, I turned and walked back to the elevator.

Not that that stopped him. 'Hey, wait a second,' he said, marching after me. 'You came all the way up here in this weather just to ask me *that*? What are you really up to? What –' Fortunately for me what sounded like a fight broke out in his apartment as the elevator door opened. As he went back to deal with it I got in the cage and jabbed the button until it started to drop me back towards the ground and the long walk home.

It was either that or drive. And I'd had enough of driving.

Driving had made me sore.

Ironically, I think that was the real reason I'd always held off learning, an irrational fear that I'd meet my maker whilst behind the wheel, come face-to-face with The Grim Reaper in all his hooded, scythe-swinging glory; whereas in reality I'd ended up with a hook-nosed Budgie, a weirdo coughing his guts up in a side street who I thought was leading me to better things despite clear evidence to the contrary and a Toucan sneezing on a metal staircase. Yet here I still was – just.

And the *real* irony? Had I not been so mentally and physically out of shape and checked the Toucan out in the first place, none of it would've happened.

So no car for me. I'd managed perfectly well without driving before, and I would do again. And god knows I needed the exercise.

Outside, the snow was falling even heavier now, the earlier flurries frozen down to a glass-like sheen on the sidewalks. Pulling up my collar and lowering my hat over my eyes, I started the long walk home, taking baby steps all the way in case I slipped and broke something else.

By the time I got home I was exhausted, but as usual lately I didn't sleep well. I keep having this nightmare where I'm flying through the cold night air surrounded by small, sparkling chips of glass, only waking up just as I'm about to hit the tarmac, my fur drenched in sweat.

No, these days walking suits me just fine.

Suits me right down to the ground.

Despite feeling less than great the next morning I made the decision to brave the weather and head in to the office, an idea slightly more appealing than sitting alone in my apartment. But half an hour into my journey I began to regret it. During the night there'd been a fresh fall of snow, and, thanks to a further drop in temperature the pavements were covered in black ice, meaning I didn't get to the office until after lunchtime. It's fair to say that when I saw Taki sitting at her desk I was as surprised to see her as she was me.

It was even more of a surprise an hour or so later when the phone rang.

As she had been doing ever since I came back, Taki picked it up before I had the chance. '*What?*' she answered, her voice loud enough to reach me through the closed door. 'Sorry, you'll have to sp- yes, yes he is here, but with the weather like it is I don't know for how much l –'

Unnerved by her unfinished sentence, I was about to call out to her when she popped her head around the door.

'Whew! That was an odd one,' she said, rubbing her paws together against the cold.

'Odd how?'

'Well, they sounded strange. *Really* strange. Like they weren't talking with their mouth.' Realising how that sounded she tried to laugh, but not very successfully. 'I mean, it *could've* been a client... then again it could've been a crank, I don't know. They asked for you by name, at any rate.'

'If it's important they'll call back. If they don't ring in the next hour it can wait until tomorrow. In fact, if you want to go now –'

'I wouldn't mind, the buses being what they are. I'll just finish up here first.' She paused. 'You – won't be long behind me, will you? I mean, if you're not, you know, dr –'

'No, I won't be long,' I promised, smiling despite myself. 'An hour and that'll be me.'

That next hour – or forty-five minutes as it turned out – passed incredibly slowly. Unable to concentrate on anything significant – not that there was anything significant that required my attention – I spent most of the time looking out of the window watching the darkness closing in around me. After about forty of those minutes the main door to the building slammed four floors below, the resultant *bang* causing one of the icicles hanging above my window to snap off and break on the sill, making me flinch. Turning back to my desk, I could hear Taki tidying up next door, readying herself to go home. Realising that as soon as she left I'd be as alone here as I would be at home, I decided to go myself. Maybe if I asked nicely she'd let me walk with her to the depot, buy her a coffee while she waited for her bus. Then I could go and get a bite to eat somewhere if anywhere was still open. Feeling slightly better, I sat on the edge of my seat, waiting until the main door opened before making my move.

Then it came.

'Okay,' she called out, 'I'm done. I'll see you tomorrow. Remember, don't stay too long because –'

Instead of finishing her sentence she let out a little cry followed by an apology. 'I'm sorry, I didn't see you there,' she said, sounding uncharacteristically flustered. 'Can I help you?'

Whatever was said next was in a voice too low for me to hear, soon followed by the *tap-tap, tap-tap* of her heels marching towards my door.

'I'll – just go and ask him,' I heard her say.

'Something wrong?' I asked as she popped her head round the door.

'No, of course not. That, um, that caller from earlier,' she gulped, looking behind her for a moment, 'they're here.'

I sighed. 'What, now? Well, I suppose you'd better show them in. It's not as if we can afford to turn the work away.'

She blinked at me for a few seconds before replying. 'No,' she said. 'No, that's right. I'll… see you in the morning.' Turning, she headed back to the anteroom, her heels skittering across the floor. Mumbling a reply to our visitor she left, slamming the outer door shut behind her.

Not wanting to appear too eager I sat back in my seat waiting for the knock at my door, the silhouette to appear on the frosted glass; but ten, twenty seconds later there was nothing. Straining my ears I listened for footsteps, but heard none. Reluctantly I began to get up from my chair, but then I heard something, or imagined I did – a faint, wet slithering noise, making its way slowly towards the door; then, very slowly, the door began to ease open but still nobody appeared, and the noise that I now knew wasn't my imagination grew even louder, becoming more unpalatable with every passing second, filling my head until I couldn't stand it any longer; then as I was about to jump from my chair and slam the door closed, I finally saw the tip of what was pushing the door inwards, perhaps a foot or so above the ground. With the gorge rising in my throat and my pulses hammering, I could only watch as the rest of it oozed its way over the threshold.

And then it spoke.

'Benji Spriteman?' it said, its voice a horrible, glutinous drawl. Nodding and gulping several times, I looked into what I hoped were its eyes, into what I hoped was its face.

'Yes. How – how can I help you?' I asked.

'Well, you see Mr Spriteman,' it said in its clogged voice as it made its way across the floor, 'it's like this…' And, after raising its shapeless, glistening bulk off the floor to a height of perhaps four feet and slopping itself down roughly in the visitor's chair, I did my best to ignore the goo dripping from its body and listened to what it had to tell me.

Later.

For the longest time I wanted it to be later, a later where I was alive, a later where I wouldn't have time to think because life would be one long rollercoaster ride, a headlong rush into the wind that threatened to rip the fur from my body, a later where I'd be hanging on by the skin of my teeth and loving every second of it.

Later.

And then, out of the blue, that later came along.

Be careful what you wish for.

Yeah, it's funny how things work out sometimes. Still, I'll be okay.

I hope.

ACKNOWLEDGEMENTS

Thank you to the following people: Stuart Young for pointing me in the direction of a superb box set which helped to confirm, strengthen and expand some of my views on all things Noir; Allyson Bird and her neighbour Penny for the information on goats; Mum, Sharon and Peter McAuley for reading the book in its raw state; Charlie the dog, for providing the basis of a character that ended up being nothing like him; the ginger Curl (name unknown) I used to see around from time to time who may or may not be like the character I created; the lady with the glamourous name I met in the doctors' not long after starting the novel; and a man from my childhood who I never met but whose name and (perhaps) reputation has stuck with me ever since.

Unlike *The Terror and the Tortoiseshell* and *The Designated Coconut* there isn't really any music in this book, but this hasn't stopped innumerable bands and individuals from providing me with literary inspiration, whether directly (Galaxie 500) or indirectly (The Minutemen). I tip my hat to all of you.

A huge thank you to writer, publisher and fellow music fan Andrew Hook for also taking a chance on me, and to Shu Yamamoto for his truly gorgeous artwork.

Finally, over the course of a lifetime you inevitably meet a lot of extremely unpleasant people and very often little can be done about them – but thankfully as a writer you can put them to good use. With this in mind, I can only say what a pleasure it's been bumping off a few of them within the pages of this book. Through gritted teeth I offer my thanks.

Last and definitely least, to the four foot high stuffed giraffe I saw outside our back door around midnight one evening shortly after watching a programme on serial killers. You scared the bejeezus out of me at the time, but I see now you might have had your uses after all. May you and your broken neck be stuck in the back of a charity shop somewhere, your black, staring glassy eyes filmed over with dust.

ABOUT THE AUTHOR

Called 'a writer of considerable energy' in *The Encyclopedia of Science Fiction,* John Travis is the author of six books – two short story collections, *Mostly Monochrome Stories* and *Gaseous Clay and Other Ambivalent Tales;* two novellas *Greenbeard* and *Eloquent Years of Silence;* and two previous Benji Spriteman novels, *The Terror and the Tortoiseshell* and *The Designated Coconut,* the former attracting the attention of several Hollywood film companies. His many short stories and novellas have been published in anthologies and journals such as *Terror Tales of Northwest England, Nemonymous, British Invasion* and in both volumes of *The Humdrumming Books of Horror Stories,* his story from the second volume, 'The Tobacconist's Concession' appearing on the 2009 shortlist for a British Fantasy Award. He's also had his work praised by TED Klein and David Renwick, and had an invisible poem read out on Radio 1 by John Hegley. Writing what he can, when he can, if by some miracle he ever *did* make any money from his stories about talking animals and various haunted objects and people, he'd like to move to the country or the coast, possibly Scarborough, and live in a detached house surrounded by books, films and musical instruments.